Half a Life

The air was hot and stale inside. Looking out from the bedroom window, through wire netting and dead insects, at the rough garden and the tall paw-paw trees and the land falling away past groves of cashews and clusters of grass roofs to the rock cones which in the distance appeared to make a continuous low pale-blue range, Willie thought, 'I don't know where I am. I don't think I can pick my way back. I don't ever want this view to become familiar. I must not unpack. I must never behave as though I am staying.'

V. S. NAIPAUL was born in Trinidad in 1932. He went to England on a scholarship in 1950. After four years at University College, Oxford, he began to write, and since then has followed no other profession. He has published more than twenty books of fiction and non-fiction, including *Half a Life*, *A House for Mr Biswas*, *A Bend in the River* and most recently *The Masque of Africa*, and a collection of correspondence, *Letters Between a Father and Son*. In 2001 he was awarded the Nobel Prize in Literature.

ALSO BY V. S. NAIPAUL

FICTION

The Mystic Masseur
The Suffrage of Elvira
Miguel Street
A House for Mr Biswas
Mr Stone and the Knights Companion
The Mimic Men
A Flag on the Island
Guerrillas
A Bend in the River
The Enigma of Arrival
A Way in the World
Magic Seeds
In a Free State

NON-FICTION

The Middle Passage
An Area of Darkness
The Loss of El Dorado
The Overcrowded Barracoon
India: A Wounded Civilization
The Return of Eva Perón
Among the Believers: An Islamic Journey
Finding the Centre
A Turn in the South
India: A Million Mutinies Now
Beyond Belief
Letters Between a Father and Son
The Writer and the World: Essays
Literary Occasions
A Writer's People: Ways of Looking and Feeling
The Masque of Africa

Half a Life

A NOVEL

V. S. NAIPAUL

PICADOR

First published 2001 by Picador

First published in paperback 2002 by Picador

This edition published 2011 by Picador
an imprint of Pan Macmillan, a division of Macmillan Publishers Limited
Pan Macmillan, 20 New Wharf Road, London N1 9RR
Basingstoke and Oxford
Associated companies throughout the world
www.panmacmillan.com

ISBN 978-0-330-52285-4

3 5 7 9 8 6 4 2

A CIP catalogue record for this book is available from
the British Library.

Typset by Intype London Ltd
Printed and bound by CPI Group (UK) Ltd, Croydon, CR0 4YY

Preface

I FELT, when I had finished *The Enigma of Arrival*, that I had come to the end of the fiction material I had inside me. The reader might feel that I say this too often, and yet the career goes on. But my feeling of emptiness at the end of *The Enigma* was quite profound. I have said elsewhere that my writing of fiction enabled me to see my life in segments. At the end of *The Enigma* there were no further segments to be explored; my material had as it were been brought up to date with my life, and there were no further segments to be explored. There remained, however, a note I had made fifteen or twenty years before. It had been done on the typewriter in small letters, in single space, and it filled a quarter page. It was the only capital that remained to me, and I began almost idly to turn this note into a book. I never expected it to go very far, but it did. And something strange happened. Having shed old themes and old ideas, it was as though there came to the writing a freshness; it was as though I had been given a second wind. I had worried, with other books, about the invention holding up. But that anxiety didn't touch me now. The humour never flagged, and my fancy roamed free. The new book was set in India, England, Portuguese Africa. This should have been taxing; but I never felt it a strain. The initial idea was quite a wicked one. A royal servant, a university student, a man of caste, decides one day to be a full Gandhian. He thinks it behoves him as a Gandhian to marry an unfortunate woman and give her a hand up, make her his equal.

There is someone at the university he has his eye on, a woman of low caste, who is also a student, in the Gandhian scheme – this kind of sacrifice on the part of the man should have led to bliss and fulfilment of some sort. In fact, it turns out to be a mess, and the troubles feed into the subsequent generation.

Willie, the son and the book's central character, goes to London; it is the only positive result of his father's bad marriage. It is 1958; there are racial disturbances in Notting Hill Gate; Willie observes them from a distance; it is his way, to keep the world at a distance. Inevitably though, Willie gets drawn into the cultural life of the capital; his horizons widen. He meets a girl from Portuguese Africa. He is attracted to her and when they get married he can only think of following her to her African home. In fact the girl's position in Africa is not as secure as Willie thinks and so Willie, of uncertain cultural inheritance, drifts further and further away. He feels himself drowning. Africa is big and overwhelming, but Willie's life there, for all its spaciousness, is unrooted and vague. It is as though he always comes back to his bad inheritance, as though that cannot be denied.

At last one day he decides to leave his wife, he tells her it is not satisfactory for him to be living her life, which for all the glamour of the early days he now sees as a colonial shadow. She says that her life tires her too; she doesn't feel that it fits her; it is really somebody else's life. The book shuts with this snappy exchange which might encourage some people to think of the narrative only as a short story, ignoring all the invention that has gone before in India and London. The illumination at the end of the book is that both Willie and his wife – to whom for many years he clung for emotional support – are also living half a life.

This book is an invention.

It is not exact about the countries, periods

or situations it appears to describe.

N. K. N.

ONE

A Visit from Somerset Maugham

WILLIE CHANDRAN asked his father one day, 'Why is my middle name Somerset? The boys at school have just found out, and they are mocking me.'

His father said without joy, 'You were named after a great English writer. I am sure you have seen his books about the house.'

'But I haven't read them. Did you admire him so much?'

'I am not sure. Listen, and make up your own mind.'

And this was the story Willie Chandran's father began to tell. It took a long time. The story changed as Willie grew up. Things were added, and by the time Willie left India to go to England this was the story he had heard.

* * *

THE WRITER (Willie Chandran's father said) came to India to get material for a novel about spirituality. This was in the 1930s. The principal of the maharaja's college brought him to me. I was doing penance for something I had done, and I was living as a mendicant in the outer courtyard of the big temple. It was a very public place, and that was why I had chosen it. My enemies among the maharaja's officials were hounding me, and I felt safer there in the temple courtyard, with the crowds coming and going, than in my office. I was in a state of nerves because of this persecution, and to calm myself I had also taken a vow of silence. This had won me a certain amount of local respect, even renown. People would come to look at me being silent and some would bring me gifts. The state authorities had to respect my vow, and my first thought when I saw the principal with the little old white fellow was that it was a plot to make me talk. This made me very obstinate. People knew that something was afoot and they stood around to watch the encounter. I knew they were on my side. I didn't say anything. The principal and the writer did all the talking. They talked about me and they looked at me while they talked, and I sat and looked through them like someone deaf and blind, and the crowd looked at all three of us.

That was how it began. I said nothing to the great man. It's hard to credit now, but I don't believe I had heard about him when I first saw him. The English literature I knew about was Browning and Shelley and people like that, whom I had studied at the university, for the year or so I was there, before I foolishly gave up English education in response to the mahatma's call, and unfitted myself for life, while watching my friends and enemies growing in prosperity and regard. That, though, is something else. I will tell you about it some other time.

Now I want to go back to the writer. You must believe

that I had said nothing to him at all. But then, perhaps eighteen months later, in the travel book the writer brought out there were two or three pages about me. There was a lot more about the temple and the crowds and the clothes they were wearing, and the gifts of coconut and flour and rice they had brought, and the afternoon light on the old stones of the courtyard. Everything the maharaja's headmaster had told him was there, and a few other things besides. Clearly the headmaster had tried to win the admiration of the writer by saying very good things about my various vows of denial. There were also a few lines, perhaps a whole paragraph, describing – in the way he had described the stones and the afternoon light – the serenity and smoothness of my skin.

That was how I became famous. Not in India, where there is a lot of jealousy, but abroad. And the jealousy turned to rage when the writer's famous novel came out during the war, and foreign critics began to see in me the spiritual source of The Razor's Edge.

My persecution stopped. The writer – to the general surprise, an anti-imperialist – had, in his first Indian book, the book of travel notes, written flatteringly of the maharaja and his state and his officials, including the principal of the college. So the attitude of everybody changed. They pretended to see me as the writer had seen me: the man of high caste, high in the maharaja's revenue service, from a line of people who had performed sacred rituals for the ruler, turning his back on a glittering career, and living as a mendicant on the alms of the poorest of the poor.

It became hard for me to step out of that role. One day the maharaja himself sent me his good wishes by one of the

Half a Life

palace secretaries. This worried me a lot. I had been hoping that after a time there might be other religious excitements in the city, and I would be allowed to go away, and work out my own way of life. But when during an important religious festival the maharaja himself came barebacked in the hot afternoon sun as a kind of penitent and with his own hand made me offerings of coconuts and cloth which a liveried courtier – a scoundrel whom I knew only too well – had brought, I recognised that breaking out had become impossible, and I settled down to live the strange life that fate had bestowed on me.

I began to attract visitors from abroad. They were principally friends of the famous writer. They came from England to find what the writer had found. They came with letters from the writer. Sometimes they came with letters from the maharaja's high officials. Sometimes they came with letters from people who had previously visited me. Some of them were writers, and months or weeks after they had visited there were little articles about their visits in the London magazines. With these visitors I went over this new version of my life so often that I became quite at ease with it. Sometimes we talked about the people who had visited, and the people with me would say with satisfaction, 'I know him. He's a very good friend.' Or words like that. So that for five months, from November to March, the time of our winter or 'cold weather', as the English people said, to distinguish the Indian season from the English season, I felt I had become a social figure, someone at the periphery of a little foreign web of acquaintances and gossip.

It sometimes happens that when you make a slip of the

[4]

tongue you don't want to correct it. You try to pretend that what you said was what you meant. And then it often happens that you begin to see that there is some truth in your error. You begin to see, for instance, that to subtract from someone's good name can also be said to detract from that name. In some such way, contemplating the strange life that had been forced on me by that meeting with the great English writer, I began to see that it was a way of life that for some years I had been dreaming of: the wish to renounce, hide, run away from the mess I had made of my life.

I must go back. We come from a line of priests. We were attached to a certain temple. I do not know when the temple was built or which ruler built it or for how long we have been attached to it; we are not people with that kind of knowledge. We of the temple priesthood and our families made a community. At one time I suppose we would have been a very rich and prosperous community, served in various ways by the people whom we served. But when the Muslims conquered the land we all became poor. The people we served could no longer support us. Things became worse when the British came. There was law, but the population increased. There were far too many of us in the temple community. This was what my grandfather told me. All the complicated rules of the community held, but there was actually very little to eat. People became thin and weak and fell ill easily. What a fate for our priestly community! I didn't like hearing the stories my grandfather told of that time, in the 1890s.

My grandfather was skin and bones when he decided he had to leave the temple and the community. He thought he would go to the big town where the maharaja's palace was and where there was a famous temple. He made such preparations as he could, saving up little portions of rice and flour and oil, and putting aside one small coin and then another. He told no one anything. When the day came he got up very early, in the dark, and began to walk to where the railway station was. It was very many miles away. He walked for three days. He walked among people who were very poor. He was more wretched than most of them, but there were people who saw that he was a starving young priest and offered him alms and shelter. At last he came to the railway station. He told me that he was by this time so frightened and lost, so close to the end of his strength and courage, that he was noticing nothing of the world outside. The train came in the afternoon. He had a memory of crowd and noise, and then it was night. He had never travelled by train before, but all the time he was looking inwards.

In the morning they came to the big town. He asked his way to the big temple and he stayed there, moving about the temple courtyard to avoid the sun. In the evening, after the temple prayers, there was a distribution of consecrated food. He was not left out of that. It was not a great deal, but it was more than he had been living on. He tried to behave as though he were a pilgrim. No one asked questions, and that was the way he lived for the first few days. But then he was noticed. He was questioned. He told his story. The temple officials didn't throw him out. It was one of these officials, a kindly man, who suggested to my grandfather that he could become a letter-writer. He provided the simple equipment, the pen and nibs and ink and paper, and my grandfather went and sat with the other letter-writers on the pavement outside the courts near the maharaja's palace.

Most of the letter-writers there wrote in English. They did petitions of various sorts for people, and helped with various government forms. My grandfather knew no English. He knew Hindi and the language of his region. There were many people in the town who had run away from the famine area and wanted to get news to their families. So there was work for my grandfather and no one was jealous of him. People were also attracted to him because of the priestly clothes he wore. He was able after a while to make a fair living. He gave up skulking about the temple courtyard in the evenings. He found a proper room, and he sent for his family. With his letter-writing work, and with his friendships at the temple, he got to know more and more people, and so in time he was able to get a respectable job as a clerk in the maharaja's palace.

That kind of job was secure. The pay wasn't very good, but nobody ever got dismissed, and people treated you with regard. My father fell easily into that way of life. He learned English and got his diplomas from the secondary school, and was soon much higher in the government than his father. He became one of the maharaja's secretaries. There were very many of those. They wore an impressive livery, and in the town they were treated like little gods. I believe my father wished me to continue in that way, to continue the climb he had begun. For my father it was as though he had rediscovered something of the security of the temple community from which my grandfather had had to flee.

But there was some little imp of rebellion in me. Perhaps

I had heard my grandfather tell too often of his flight and his fear of the unknown, only looking inward during those terrible days and not able to see what was around him. My grandfather grew angrier as he grew older. He said then that in his temple community they had been very foolish. They had seen the disaster coming but had done nothing about it. He himself, he said, had left it to the last moment to run away; which was why, when he came to the big town, he had had to skulk about the temple courtyard like a half-starved animal. These were terrible words for him to use. His anger infected me. I began to have some idea that this life we were all living in the big town around the maharaja and his palace couldn't last, that this security was also false. When I thought like that I could panic, because I couldn't see what I could do to protect myself against that breakdown.

I suppose I was ripe for political action. India was full of politics. But the independence movement didn't exist in the maharaja's state. It was illegal. And though we knew of the great names and the great doings outside we saw them at a distance.

I was now at the university. The plan was that I should get a BA degree and then perhaps get a scholarship from the maharaja to do medicine or engineering. Then I was to marry the daughter of the principal of the maharaja's college. All of that was settled. I let it happen, but felt detached from it. I became idler and idler at the university. I didn't understand the BA course. I didn't understand *The Mayor of Casterbridge*. I couldn't understand the people or the story and didn't know what period the book was set in. Shakespeare was better, but I didn't know what to make of Shelley and Keats and

Wordsworth. When I read those poets I wanted to say, 'But this is just a pack of lies. No one feels like that.' The professor made us copy down his notes. He dictated them, pages and pages, and what I mainly remember is that, because he was dictating notes and wanted them to be brief, and because he wanted us to copy down these notes exactly, he never spoke the name Wordsworth. He always said W, speaking just the initial, never Wordsworth. W did this, W wrote that.

I was in a great mess, feeling that we were all living in a false security, feeling idle, hating my studies, and knowing that great things were happening outside. I adored the great names of the independence movement. I felt rebuked in my idleness, and in the servility of the life that was being prepared for me. And when sometime in 1931 or 1932 I heard that the mahatma had called for students to boycott their universities, I decided to follow the call. I did more. In the front yard I made a little bonfire of *The Mayor of Casterbridge* and Shelley and Keats, and the professor's notes, and went home to wait for the storm to beat about my head.

Nothing happened. Nobody seemed to have told my father anything. No message came from the dean. Perhaps it hadn't been much of a bonfire. Books aren't so easy to burn, unless you have a good fire already going. And it was possible that in the untidiness and noise of the university front yard, with the life of the street just there, what I was doing in a little corner mightn't have seemed so strange.

I felt more useless than ever. In other parts of India there were great men. To be able to follow those great men, even to catch a sight of them, would have been bliss for me. I would have given anything to be in touch with their greatness.

Here there was only the servile life around the palace of the maharaja. Night after night I debated what I should do. The mahatma himself, I knew, had gone through a crisis like this only a year or two before in his ashram. Apparently at peace there, living a life of routine, adored by everyone around him, he had actually been worrying, to a pitch of torment, how he might set the country alight. And he had come up with the unexpected and miraculous idea of the Salt March, a long march from his ashram to the sea, to make salt.

So, living securely at home, in the house of my father the courtier in livery, still (for the sake of peace) pretending to attend the university, but tormented in the way I have said, I at last felt inspiration touch me. I felt with every kind of certainty that the decision that had come to me was just, and I was determined to carry it through. The decision was nothing less than to make a sacrifice of myself. Not an empty sacrifice, the act of a moment – any fool can jump off a bridge or throw himself in front of a train – but a more lasting kind of sacrifice, something the mahatma would have approved of. He had spoken much about the evils of casteism. No one had said he was wrong, but very few had done anything about it.

My decision was simple. It was to turn my back on our ancestry, the foolish, foreign-ruled starveling priests my grandfather had told me about, to turn my back on all my father's foolish hopes for me as someone high in the maharaja's service, all the foolish hopes of the college principal to have me marry his daughter. My decision was to turn my back on all those ways of death, to trample on them, and to do the only noble thing that lay in my power, which was to marry the lowest person I could find.

I actually had someone in mind. There was a girl at the university. I didn't know her. I hadn't spoken to her. I had merely noticed her. She was small and coarse-featured, almost tribal in appearance, noticeably black, with two big top teeth that showed very white. She wore colours that were sometimes very bright and sometimes very muddy, seeming to run into the blackness of her skin. She would have belonged to a backward caste. The maharaja gave a certain number of scholarships to 'the backwards', as they were called. The maharaja was known for his piety, and this giving of scholarships was one of his acts of religious charity. That, in fact, was my first thought when I saw the girl in the lecture room with her books and papers. A lot of people were looking at her. She wasn't looking at anyone. I saw her often after that. She held her pen in a strange, determined, childish way, and copied down the professor's notes about Shelley and W, of course, and Browning and Arnold and the importance in *Hamlet* of soliloquy.

The last word gave us a lot of trouble. The professor pronounced it in three or four different ways, according to his mood; and when he was testing our knowledge of his notes, and we had to speak the word, it was, you might say, every man for himself. Literature for many of us was this kind of confusion. I thought for some reason that the scholarship girl, since she was a scholarship girl, understood more than most of us. But then one day when the professor asked her a question – normally he didn't pay her too much attention – I saw that she understood a good deal less. She had almost no idea of the story of *Hamlet*. All she had been learning were words. She had thought that the play was set in India. It was easy for the professor to mock her, and people in the class laughed, as though they knew much more.

I began after this to pay more attention to the girl. I was fascinated and repelled by her. She would have been of the very low. It would have been unbearable to consider her family and clan and their occupations. When people like that went to the temple they would have been kept out of the sanctum, the inner cell with the image of the deity. The officiating priest would never have wanted to touch those people. He would have thrown the sacred ash at them, the way food is thrown to a dog. All kinds of ideas like that came to me when I contemplated the scholarship girl, who felt people's eyes on her and never returned their gaze. She was trying to keep her end up. It would have taken so little to crush her. And gradually, with my fascination, there came a little sympathy, a wish to look at the world through her eyes.

This was the girl I thought I should go and make a declaration to and in her company live out a life of sacrifice.

There was a tea-room or restaurant the students went to. We called it a hotel. It was in a lane off the main road. It was very cheap. When you asked the waiter for cigarettes he placed an open pack of five on the table, and you paid only for what you took. It was there one day that I saw the scholarship girl, alone in her muddy clothes at the little ring-marked table below the ceiling fan. I went and sat at her table. She should have looked pleased, but she looked frightened. And then I understood that though I might have known who she was, she perhaps had not looked at me. In the BA class I was not that distinctive.

So right at the beginning there was this little warning. I noted it, but I didn't heed it.

I said to her, 'I've seen you in the English class.' I wasn't sure this was the right thing to say. It might have made her feel I had witnessed her humiliation when the professor had tried to get her to talk about *Hamlet*. She didn't say anything. The thin, shiny-faced waiter, in the very dirty white jacket he had worn for days, came and put a dripping glass of water on the table and asked what I wanted. That eased the embarrassment of the moment for me. But not for her. She was in a strange situation, and she was being witnessed. Her very dark top lip slipped slowly – with the wetness of a snail, I thought – over her big white teeth. For the first time I saw that she used powder. There was a thin white bloom on her cheeks and forehead; it made the black skin matt, and you could see where the powder ended and the shiny skin showed again. I was repelled, ashamed, moved.

I didn't know what to talk about. I couldn't say, 'Where do you live? What does your father do? Do you have brothers? What do they do?' All of those questions would have caused trouble and, to tell the truth, I didn't want to know the answers. The answers would have taken me down into a pit. I didn't want to go there. So I sat and sipped at the coffee and smoked a thin cheap cigarette from the pack of five the waiter put down for me and said nothing. Looking down I caught sight of her thin black feet in her cheap slippers, and again I was surprised at how moved I was.

I took to going to the tea-shop as often as I could and

whenever I saw the girl there I sat at her table. We didn't talk. One day she came in after me. She didn't come to my table. I was in a quandary. I considered the other people in the tea-shop, people with ordinary and secure lives ahead of them, and for a long minute or two I was, to tell the truth, a little frightened, and thought of giving up the idea of the life of sacrifice. I could simply have stayed at my table. But then, nagged by some feeling of failure and some irritation at the scholarship girl's indifference, I went and sat at her table. She seemed to expect it, and seemed very slightly to move to one side, as if making room for me.

That was how it was that term. No words spoken, no meeting of any sort outside the tea-shop, yet a special kind of relationship established. We began to get strange looks in the tea-shop, and I began to get those looks even when I was on my own. The girl was mortified. I could see that she didn't know how to deal with those judging eyes. But what mortified her gave me a strange satisfaction. I looked upon that kind of judgement – from waiters, students, simple people – as the first sweet fruit of my life of sacrifice. They were only the first fruits. I knew that there were going to be greater battles ahead, severer tests, and even sweeter fruit.

The first of those battles was not long in coming. One day in the tea-room the girl spoke to me. I had got used to the silence between us – it seemed a perfect way of communication – and this forwardness in someone I had thought of as backward took me by surprise. Mixed up with this surprise was my dismay at her voice. I realised then that in the class, even at the time of her trouble with the professor over *Hamlet*, I had only heard her mumble. Her voice, heard in this intimate way across the little square tea-table, was not soft and shy and aiming at sweetness, as you might have expected from someone so small and slight and diffident, but loud and coarse and rasping. It was the kind of voice I associated with people of her kind. I thought it might have been something that as a scholarship girl she had left behind.

I hated that voice as soon as I heard it. I felt, not for the first time, that I was sinking. But that was the terror that went with the life of sacrifice I had committed myself to, and I felt I had absolutely to go ahead.

I was so preoccupied with these thoughts – her forwardness, the hatefulness of her voice (like an expression of her big white top teeth and her powdered dark skin), my fear for myself – that I had to ask her to say again what she had said.

She said, 'Somebody has told my uncle.'

Uncle? I felt she had no right to be dragging me into these unsavoury depths. Who was this uncle? What hole did he live in? Even the word 'uncle' – which was a word that other people used of a sometimes precious relationship – was presumptuous.

I said, 'Who is this uncle?'

'He is with the Labourers Union. A *firebrand*.'

She used the English word, and it sounded very strange and acrid in her mouth. We didn't have nationalist politics in the state – it wasn't allowed by the maharaja – but we did have this semi-nationalist subterfuge, which found pretty words, like 'labourers' or 'workers', for the uglier words that were in everyday use. And, all at once, I knew who she might be. She would have been related to the firebrand, and this would have explained her getting the scholarship from the maharaja. In her own eyes she was a person of power and influence, someone on the rise.

She said, 'He says he is going to take out a procession against you. Caste oppression.'

That would have suited me down to the ground. It would have made a public statement of my rejection of old values. It would have broadcast my adherence to the ideas of the mahatma, my life of sacrifice.

She said, 'He says he is going to take out a procession and burn your house down. The whole world has seen you sitting with me in this tea-house week after week. What are you going to do?'

I was really frightened. I knew those firebrands. I said, 'What do you think I should do?'

'You have to hide me somewhere, until things calm down.'

I said, 'But that would be kidnapping you.'

'It is what you have to do.'

She was calm. I was like a drowning man.

A few short months before I had been an ordinary, idle young man at the university, the son of a courtier, living in my father's Grade C official house, thinking about the great men of our country and yearning to be great myself, without seeing any way, in the smallness of our life, of embarking on that career of greatness, capable only of listening to film songs, yielding to the emotion they called up, and then enfeebled by shameful private vice (about which I intend to say no more, since such things are universal), and generally feeling oppressed by the nothingness of our world and the servility of our life. Now in almost every particular my life had altered. It was as though, like a child seeing the sky reflected in a puddle after rain, I had, wishing to feel fear while knowing I was safe, let my foot touch the puddle, which at that touch had turned into a raging flood which was now sweeping me away. That was how in a few minutes I had begun to feel. And that in a few minutes became my view of the world about me: no longer a dull and ordinary place where ordinary people walked and worked, but a place where secret torrents flowed which might at any minute sweep away the unwary. It was what came to my mind now when I looked at the girl. All her attributes changed: the thin black feet, the big teeth, the very dark skin.

I had to find a place for her. It was her idea. A hotel or boarding house was out of the question. I thought of the people I knew. I had to forget family friends, university friends. I thought in the end I would try the image-maker in the town. There was an old connection between the factory and the temple of my ancestors. It was a place I had often gone to. I knew the master. He was a small dusty fellow with glasses. He looked blind, but that was because his glasses were always dusty with the chippings of his workmen. Ten or twelve of them were always there, small barebacked fellows, quite ordinary in appearance, chipping away in the yard, hammer on chisel, chisel on stone, making twenty or twenty-four separate sounds all the time. It wasn't easy to be in the middle of that noise. But I didn't think the scholarship girl would mind.

The image-makers were of a neutral caste, not low, but very far from being high, and perfect for my purpose. Many of the craftsmen lived in the master's compound with their families.

The master was working on a complicated drawing of a temple pillar. He was pleased as always to see me. I looked at his drawing, and he showed me others, and I worked the subject round to the girl, a 'backward' who had been expelled and threatened by her family and was now in need of shelter. I decided not to speak shyly, but with authority. The master knew of my ancestry. He would never have associated me with such a woman, and I suggested that I was acting on behalf of someone very high indeed. It was well known that the maharaja was sympathetic to the backwards. And the master behaved like a man who knew the ways of the world.

There was a room at the back of the storehouse where there were images and statues and busts of various sorts. The dusty little fellow with the blind glasses was gifted. He didn't do only the deities, complicated things that had to be done in a precise way; he also did real people, living and dead. He did lots of mahatmas and other giants of the nationalist movement; and he did busts (from photographs) of people's parents and grandparents. Sometimes those family busts carried the real glasses of the people. It was a place full of presences, disturbing to me after a time. It was comforting to know that every deity was flawed in some way, so that its terrible power couldn't become real and overwhelm us all.

I wished I could have left the girl there and never gone back, but there was always the threat of the firebrand, her uncle. And the longer she stayed there the harder it became for me to send her away; the more it seemed that we were together for life, though I hadn't even touched her.

I lived at home. I went out to the university and pretended to be at the lectures, and then sometimes I would go to the sculptor's yard. I never stayed long. I never wanted the master to suspect anything.

Life couldn't have been easy for her. One day, in that room without light, where the dust of the sculptor's yard coated everything, and was like a powder on the girl's skin, she seemed to me to be very melancholy.

I said, 'What's the matter?'

She said, in her terrible rough voice, 'I was thinking how my life has changed.'

I said, 'What about my life?'

She said, 'If I was outside I would be doing the exams now. Are they easy?'

I said, 'I am boycotting the university.'

'How will you get a job? Who will give you money? Go and do the exams.'

'I haven't studied. I can't learn those notes now. It is too late.'

'They will pass you. You know those people.'

When the results came out my father said, 'I can't understand it. I hear that you knew nothing at all about the Romantics and *The Mayor of Casterbridge*. They wanted to fail you. The principal of the college had to talk them out of it.'

I should have said, 'I burnt my books long ago. I am following the mahatma's call. I am boycotting English education.' But I was too weak. At a critical moment I failed myself. All I said was, 'I felt all my strength oozing out of me in the examination room.' And I could have cried at my weakness.

My father said, 'If you were having trouble with Hardy

and Wessex and so on, you should have come to me. I have all my school notes still.'

He was off duty, in the hot little front room of our Grade C house. He was without his turban and livery, only in a singlet and dhoti. The maharaja's courtiers, in spite of their turbans and livery, with day coats and night coats, never wore shoes, and my father's soles were black and callused and about half an inch thick.

He said, 'So I suppose it's the Land Tax department for you.'

And I began to work for the maharaja's state. The Land Tax department was very big. Everybody who owned any little piece of land had to pay an annual tax on it. There were officers all over the state surveying the land, recording ownership, collecting the tax, and keeping accounts. My job was in the central office. It was a pretty building in white marble and it had a high dome. It was full of rooms. I worked with twenty others in a big, high room. It was full of papers on desks and on deep shelves like those in the left-luggage rooms in railway stations. The papers were in cardboard folders tied with string; sometimes they were in bundles wrapped in cloth. The folders in the top shelves, many years old, were dingy with dust and cigarette smoke. The ceiling was brown with this smoke. The room was nicotine-brown at the top, dark-mahogany lower down, on the doors, desks, and floor.

I grieved for myself. This kind of servile labour had formed no part of my vision of the life of sacrifice. But now I was glad to have it. I needed the money, paltry though it was. I was deep in debt. I had used my father's name and position in the palace and taken money from various money-lenders to support the girl in the room at the image-maker's.

She had made the place presentable. That had cost money; and then there had been the kitchen paraphernalia, and her clothes. So I had been having all the expenses of a married man, and living like an ascetic in my father's Grade C house.

The girl never believed I didn't have the money. She believed that people of my background had secret funds. It was part of the propaganda outside against our caste, and I endured what was said without comment. Whenever I took her another little piece of money from a moneylender she didn't look surprised. She might say, with irony (or sarcasm: I don't know what our professor would have said), 'You look very sad. But your caste always look sad when they give.' She sometimes had the style of her uncle, the firebrand of the backwards.

I was full of grief. But she was happy about the new job.

She said, 'I must say it would be nice to get some regular money for a change.'

I said, 'I don't know how long I can last in that job.'

She said, 'I've put up with a lot of hardship already. I don't intend to put up with much more. I could have been a BA. If you hadn't taken me away from the university I would have done the exam. My family went to a lot of trouble to send me to the university.'

I could have wept with rage.

Not so much at what she was saying, but at the idea of the prison-house in which I now had to live. Day after day I left my father's house and went to work. I felt like a child again. There was a story which my father and mother used to tell people about me when I was a child. They had said to me one day, 'Today we are going to take you to school.' At the end of the day they asked me, 'Did you like school?' I said, 'I loved it.' The next morning they got me up early. When I asked why they were doing that they said, 'You have to go to school.' And I said, crying, 'But I went to school yesterday.' That was the way I felt about going to work in the Land Tax department, and the thought of going to work in a place like that every day every year until I died frightened me.

One day in the office the supervisor came and said, 'You are being transferred to the audit section.'

In that section we had to look out for corruption among the tax-collectors and surveyors. Officers would take the land tax from poor people who couldn't read, and not give receipts, and the poor peasant with his three or four acres would have to pay the tax again. Or he would have to pay a bribe to get his receipt. It was endless, the petty cheating that went on among the poor. The officers were not much richer than the peasants. Who was suffering when the tax was not paid? The more I looked at these dirty pieces of paper the more I found myself on the side of the cheats. I began to destroy or throw away those damning little pieces of paper. I became a kind of saboteur, and it gave me great pleasure to think that in this office, without making any big statement, I was conducting my own kind of civil disobedience.

The supervisor said to me one day, 'The Chief Inspector wants to see you.'

My bravery vanished. I thought of the debts, the money-lender, the girl in the room at the image-maker's.

The Chief Inspector sat at a desk and was surrounded by his own files, files of ill-doing that had been sifted at half a dozen desks and then sifted again and had at last arrived here, for this man's awful judgement.

He rocked back on his chair, looking at me through his thick-lensed glasses, and said, 'Are you happy with your work here?'

I bowed my head. I didn't say anything.

He said, 'From next week you will be an Assistant Inspector.'

It was a big promotion. I felt it was a trap. I said, 'I don't know, sir. I don't feel I have the qualifications.'

He said, 'We are not making you a full Inspector. We are only making you an Assistant Inspector.'

It was the first of my promotions. It didn't matter how badly I did my job, how much I sabotaged, they continued to promote me. It was like civil disobedience in reverse.

It worried me. I talked to my father about it one evening.

He said, 'The school principal has great ambitions for his son-in-law.'

I said, 'I can't be his son-in-law. I am already married.'

I don't know why it came to me to say that. It wasn't strictly true, of course. But that was the way I had begun to think about my relationship with the girl at the image-maker's.

My father went wild. All his tolerance and kindness disappeared. He became heart-broken. It was a very long time before he could ask me for the details.

'Who is the girl?'

I told him. He couldn't speak. I thought he was going to collapse. I wanted to calm him down. So I told him about the firebrand, the girl's uncle. I was trying to tell him, in a foolish kind of way, quite contrary to my ideas of sacrifice, that the girl had a background of some sort and wasn't a complete nobody. It made matters worse. He didn't like hearing about the firebrand. He lay down flat on an old bamboo mat on the concrete floor in our little front room, and he called for my mother. I could see very clearly the thick pads of hardened skin on the soles of his feet. They were dirty and cracked and there were little strips peeling off the side. As a courtier my father had never been allowed to wear shoes. But he had bought shoes for me.

He said at last, 'You've blackened all our faces. And now we'll have to face the anger of the school principal. You've dishonoured his daughter, since in everybody's eyes you are as good as married to her.'

So, though I hadn't touched either of them, and though I had gone through no form of ceremony with either of them, there were two women whom I had dishonoured.

In the morning my father was hollow-eyed. He had slept badly. He said, 'For centuries we have been what we are. Even when the Muslims came. Even when we starved. Now you've thrown our inheritance away.'

I said, 'Now is a time for sacrifice.'

'Sacrifice, sacrifice. Why?'

'I am following the mahatma's call.'

That made my father stop, and I said, 'I am sacrificing the only thing I have to sacrifice.' It was a line that had come to me the evening before.

My father said, 'The school principal is a powerful man, and I am sure he will be finding ways of lighting a fire under

us. I don't know how I can tell him. I don't know how I can
face him. It's easy enough for you to talk of sacrifice. You
can leave. You are young. Your mother and I will have to
live with the consequences. It will be better, in fact, if you
did leave. You wouldn't be allowed to live with a backward
here. Have you thought of that?'

And my father was right. It was easy enough for me so
far. I wasn't actually living with the woman. That idea became
daily more concrete, and it repelled me more and more. So I
was in a strange position.

For some weeks life went on as before. I lived in my
father's government house. I made occasional trips to the
image-maker's. I went to work in the Land Tax department.
My father was always worried about the school principal, but
nothing happened.

One day the messenger said to me, 'The Chief Inspector
wants to see you.'

The Chief Inspector had a pile of folders on his desk. I
recognised some of them. He said, 'If I tell you that you've
been recommended for another promotion, would it surprise
you?'

'No. Yes. But I am not qualified. I can't cope with these
promotions.'

'That's what I feel, too. I've been going through some of
your work. I am bewildered by it. Documents have been
destroyed, receipts thrown away.'

I said, 'I don't know. Some vandal.'

'I think I should tell you right away. You are being
investigated for corruption. There have been complaints by
senior officials. It's a serious matter, corruption. You can go

to jail. RI, rigorous imprisonment. There is enough in these files to convict you.'

I went to the girl at the image-maker's. She was the only person I could talk to.

She said, 'You were on the side of the cheats?' It seemed to please her.

'Well, yes. I didn't think they were ever going to find out. There's so much paper in that place. They could cook up any kind of case against anybody. The college principal is against me, I should tell you. He wanted me to marry his daughter.'

The girl understood the situation right away. I didn't have to say any more. She made all the connections.

She said, 'I will get my uncle to take out a procession.'

Uncle, procession: a mob of backwards carrying their crude banners and shouting my name outside the palace and the secretariat. I said, 'No, no. Please don't have a procession.'

She insisted. Her blood was up. She said, 'He's a *crowd-puller*.' She used the English word.

The thought of being protected by the firebrand was unbearable. And I knew that – after all the blows I had dealt him – it would have killed my father. And that was when, caught between the girl and the school principal, the firebrand and the threat of imprisonment, caught between the devil and deep blue sea in every direction, as you might say, I began to think of running away. I began to think of taking sanctuary in the famous old temple in the town. Like my grandfather. At this moment of supreme sacrifice I fell, as if by instinct, into old ways.

I made my preparations secretly. There was not much to

prepare. The hardest thing to do was to shave my head clean. And very early one morning, like the Lord Buddha leaving the revels of his father's palace, I left my father's house and, dressed like a man of my caste, I walked barefooted and barebacked to the temple. My father had never worn shoes. I had always worn them, except on certain religious occasions, and the soles of my feet were thin-skinned and soft, without my father's pads. Soon they were very tender, and I wondered what they would be like when the sun came up and the paving stones of the temple courtyard became hot.

Like my grandfather all those years ago I moved about the courtyard during the day to avoid the sun. After the prayers in the evening I was offered food. And when the time was ripe I declared myself a mendicant to the temple priests, and claimed sanctuary, letting them know my ancestry at the same time. I made no attempt to hide. The temple courtyard was as public as the main road. I thought that the more the public saw me, the more they got to know about my life of sacrifice, the greater was my security. But my case was not very well known, and it actually took some time, three or four days, for my presence in the temple to be known, and for the scandal to break out.

The school principal and the officials of the Land Tax department were about to pounce when the firebrand took out a procession. Everybody became very frightened. Nobody touched me. And that was how, to my mortification and sorrow, and with every kind of grief for my father and our past, I became part of the cause of the backwards.

This lasted for two or three weeks. I didn't know how to move, and had no idea where the whole thing was going to end. I had no idea how long I would last in that strange situation. The government lawyers were at work, and I knew that if it wasn't for the firebrand, no amount of sanctuary was going to save me from the courts. It occurred then to me to do as the mahatma had done at some stage: to take a vow of silence. It suited my temperament, and it also seemed the least complicated way out. The news of this vow of silence spread. Simple people who had come from far to pay their respects to the temple deity would now also stop off to pay their respects to me. I became at once a holy man and, because of the firebrand and his niece outside, a political cause.

My case became almost as well known as that of a scoundrelly lawyer in another state, a jumped-up backward called Madhavan. That insolent fellow — going against all custom and decency — had insisted on walking past a temple while the priests were doing a long and taxing set of religious ceremonies. If you made one small mistake during those particular ceremonies you had to go back to the beginning. On such occasions it was better for backwards with their distracting babble to be out of the way, and the whole temple street was of course closed to them.

Elsewhere in the country they were talking of Gandhi and Nehru and the British. Here in the maharaja's state they were shut off from those politics. They were half-nationalists or quarter-nationalists or less. Their big cause was the caste war. For quite a time they did civil disobedience about the lawyer and me, campaigning for the lawyer's right to walk past the temple, and for my right to marry the firebrand's niece, or for her right to marry me.

A Visit from Somerset Maugham

The processions and the one-day strikes kept me safe from the school principal and the courts, and from the girl as well. But it pained me more than I can say to be put on a par with that lawyer. I thought it unfair that my simple life of sacrifice had taken that turn. I had wished, after all, only to follow the great men of our country. Fate, tossing me about, had made me a hero to people who, fighting their own petty caste war, wished to pull them down.

For three months or so I lived in this way, accepting homage from temple visitors, not noticing their gifts, and of course never talking. It actually wasn't a disagreeable way of passing the time. It suited me. And of course in my situation the vow of silence was a great help. I had no idea where the whole thing was going to end, but after a while I stopped worrying about that. I even began, when my silence overpowered me, a little bit to enjoy the feeling of being detached, of floating, with no links to anyone or anything. Sometimes for ten or fifteen minutes or longer I forgot my situation. Sometimes I even forgot where I was.

And that was when the great writer and his friend appeared, together with the school principal, and my life took yet another turn.

The principal was also director of the state's tourist publications and sometimes showed distinguished people around. He shot me glances of pure hatred – every kind of old anxiety came back to me then – and was for passing me by, but the writer's friend, Mr Haxton, asked about me. The principal said, making an irritated, dismissing gesture with his hand, 'Nobody, nobody.' But Mr Haxton pressed, and asked why people were bringing me gifts. The principal told them I had taken a vow of silence, and had already been silent for a hundred days. The writer was very interested in that. The principal saw, and in the way of people of his kind, and as a good servant of the maharaja's tourist department, he began to say what he thought the old writer and his friend wanted to hear. He fixed his hard hating eyes on me and boasted about my priestly family and our temple ancestors. He boasted about my own early career, the bright prospects I had. All of these things I had mysteriously given away for the life of the ascetic, living in the courtyard, dependent on the bounty of pilgrims to the temple.

I was frightened of this eulogy by the principal. I thought he was plotting something nasty, and I looked away while he spoke, as though I didn't understand the language he was speaking.

The principal said, biting hard at each word, 'He fears a great punishment in this life and the next. And he is right to fear.'

The writer said, 'What do you mean?' He had a bad stammer.

The principal said, 'Aren't we all every day both paying for past sins and storing up punishment for the future? Isn't that the trap of every man? It is the only explanation I have for my own misfortunes.'

I ignored the rebuke in his voice. I didn't turn back to face him.

The writer and his friend came again the next day, without the principal. The writer said, 'I know about your vow of silence. But will you write down some answers to some questions I have?' I didn't nod or make any gesture of assent, but he asked his friend for a pad and he wrote on it in pencil, 'Are you happy?' The question mattered to me, and I took the pad and pencil and wrote, with perfect seriousness, 'Within my silence I feel quite free. That is happiness.'

There were a few more questions like that. Quite easy stuff, really, once I had got into it. The answers came to me without any trouble. I rather enjoyed it. I could see that the writer was pleased. He said to his friend, speaking quite loudly, as though because I wasn't speaking I was also deaf, 'I feel this is a little bit like Alexander and the brahmin. Do you know that story?' Mr Haxton said with irritation, 'I don't know the story.' He was red-eyed and grumpy that morning. It might have been because of the heat. It was very bright, and the bleached stone of the temple courtyard gave off a lot of heat. The writer said with an easy malice, and without a stammer, 'No matter.' Then he turned to me and we did a little more writing.

At the end of this meeting I felt I had passed an examination. I knew that word of this business would spread, and that because of the regard of the great writer, the principal and all the other officials of the state wouldn't be able to do me any harm. So it turned out. In fact, they had to start being proud of me while the writer was around. Like the poor school principal himself, they all had to start boasting about me a little bit.

In time the writer wrote his book. Then other foreign people came. And that was how, as I said earlier, even while the great independence struggle was going on outside, I began to acquire something like a reputation – modest, but nonetheless quite real – in certain quite influential intellectual or spiritual circles abroad.

There was no escaping the role now. In the beginning I felt I had trapped myself. But very soon I found that the role fitted. I became easier and easier with it, and I understood one day that, through a series of accidents, tossed as in a dream from one unlikely situation to another, acting always on the spur of the moment, wishing only to reject the servility of our life, with no clear view of what was to follow, I had fallen into ancestral ways. I was astonished and awed. I felt that some higher power had taken a hand and I had been shown the true path.

My father and the school principal thought otherwise. To them – in spite of all the praising things the principal had to say for official reasons – I was irredeemably tarnished, a fallen man of caste, and my path a mockery of sacred ways. But I let them be. They and their grief were far from me.

The time now came for me to regularise my life. I couldn't keep on living at the temple. I had in some way to set up on my own, and straighten out my life with the girl. I couldn't get away from her any more than I could give up my role. To abandon her would have been to compound the dishonour; and there was always the firebrand to reckon with. I couldn't simply say sorry to everybody and go back to what I had been.

All this while she had been living at the image-maker's, in her little lodging behind the store-room with the finished deities and the white marble dummies of important local people. Every day our association, quite famous in our town now, seemed more settled, and I grew every day more ashamed of her. I was as ashamed of her as much as my father and mother and the principal, and people of our sort generally, were ashamed of me. This shame was always with me, the little unhappiness always at the back of my mind, like an incurable illness, corrupting all my moments, all my little triumphs (another reference in a book, another magazine article, another titled visitor). I began – though it might seem strange to say so – to take refuge in my melancholy. I courted it, and lost myself in it. Melancholy became so much part of my character that for long periods I could forget the cause.

So at last I became a man with an establishment of my own. There was one little blessing. It was assumed that I was married to the girl. So there was no ceremony. I don't think I could have gone through with that. My heart would not have taken the sacrilege. Privately, in the recesses of my heart, I took a vow of sexual abstinence, a vow of *brahmacharya*. Like the mahatma. Unlike him, I failed. I was full of shame. And I was very swiftly punished. I soon afterwards had to recognise that the girl was pregnant. That pregnancy, that distending of her stomach, that alteration of her already unattractive body, tormented me, made me pray that what I was witnessing wasn't there.

All my anxiety, when little Willie was born, was to see how much of the backward could be read in his features. Anyone seeing me bend over the infant would have thought I was looking at the little creature with pride. In fact, my thoughts were all inward, and my heart was sinking.

A little later, as he started to grow up, I would look at him without saying anything and feel myself close to tears. I would think, 'Little Willie, little Willie, what have I done to you? Why have I forced this taint on you?' And then I would think, 'But that is nonsense. He is not you or yours. His face makes that plain. You have forced no taint on him. Whatever you gave him has disappeared in his wider inheritance.' But some little hope for him always stayed with me. I would, for instance, see someone of our kind and think, 'But he looks like Willie. He is the image of little Willie.' And with this hope beating in my heart I would go and look at him, and at the first glimpse I would know I had fooled myself again.

All this was a private drama. It was absorbed into my melancholy. I opened myself to no one about it. I wonder what Willie's mother would have said if she knew. With the birth of her son she came into a kind of horrible flowering. She seemed to forget the nature of my calling. She became house-proud. She took lessons in flower arrangement from the wife of an English officer – independence had not yet come: we still had a British garrison in the town – and she took lessons in cooking and housecraft from a Parsi lady. She tried to entertain my guests. I was mortified. I remember one dreadful occasion. She had set or laid out the table in her new way. On the side plate of each guest she had placed a towel. I didn't think it was right. I had never read about towels on a dining table or seen them in any of the foreign films I had gone to. She insisted. She used the word 'serviette' or something like that. She was no longer on the defensive these days, and soon she was saying foolish things about my ancestors, who knew nothing about modern housecraft. Nothing was resolved when the first guest came (a Frenchman who was doing a book about Romain Rolland, whom we all adored in India, because he was said to be an admirer of the mahatma), and I had to retreat into my melancholy, and go through the whole evening with those towels on the table.

This was the nature of my life. My utter wretchedness, my self-disgust, can be imagined when, with everything I have spoken about, and in spite of my private vow of *brahma-charya*, which represented the profoundest part of my nature, Willie's mother became pregnant for the second time. This time it was a girl, and this time there was no room for any kind of self-delusion. The girl was the image of her mother. It was like divine punishment. I called her Sarojini, after the woman poet of the independence movement, in the hope that a similar kind of blessing might fall on her, because the poet Sarojini, great patriot though she was, and much admired for that, was also remarkably ill-favoured.

* * *

THIS WAS THE STORY that Willie Chandran's father told. It took about ten years. Different things had to be said at different times. Willie Chandran grew up during the telling of this story.

His father said, 'You asked me many years ago, before I began the story, whether I really admired the writer after whom you are named. I said I wasn't sure, that you would have to make up your own mind. Now that you've heard what I had to say, what do you think?'

Willie Chandran said, 'I despise you.'

'That is your mother talking.'

Willie Chandran said, 'What is there for me in what you have said? You offer me nothing.'

His father said, 'It has been a life of sacrifice. I have no riches to offer you. All I have are my friendships. That is my treasure.'

'What about poor Sarojini?'

'I will speak to you frankly. I feel she was sent to try us. I can tell you nothing about her appearance that you don't already know. Her prospects in this country are not bright. But foreigners have their own ideas of beauty and certain other things, and all I can hope for Sarojini is an international marriage.'

TWO

The First Chapter

WILLIE CHANDRAN and his sister Sarojini went to the mission school. One day one of the Canadian teachers asked Willie, in a smiling friendly way, 'What does your father do?' It was a question he had put at various times to other boys as well, and they had all readily spoken the various degraded callings of their fathers. Willie wondered at their shamelessness. But now when the question was put to him Willie found he didn't know what to say about his father's business. He also found he was ashamed. The teacher kept on smiling, waiting for an answer, and at last Willie Chandran said with irritation, 'You all know what my father does.' The class laughed. They laughed at his irritation and not at what he had said. From that day Willie Chandran began to despise his father.

Willie Chandran's mother had been educated at the mission school, and it was her wish that her children should go there. Most of the children at the school were backwards who would not have been accepted at the local schools for people of caste, or would have found life hard if they had got in. She

[37]

herself in the beginning had gone to one of those caste schools. It was a broken-down and dusty shack in a suburb far from the maharaja's palace and all his good intentions. Broken-down though it was, the teachers and the school servants didn't want Willie Chandran's mother there. The school servants were even more fierce than the teachers. They said they would starve rather than serve in a school which took in backwards. They said they would go on strike. Somehow in the end they all swallowed their pride and their talk of going on strike, and the girl was allowed in. Things went wrong on the first day. In the morning recess the girl ran with the other children to the place in the schoolyard where a ragged and half-starved school servant was giving out water from a barrel. He used a long-handled bamboo dipper and when a student appeared before him he poured water into a brass vessel or an aluminium one. Willie Chandran's mother wondered in a childish way whether she would get brass or aluminium. But when she appeared before him no choice like that was offered her. The ragged half-starved man became very angry and frightening and made the kind of noise he would have made before he beat a stray dog. Some of the children objected, and then the water man made a show of looking for something and from somewhere on the ground he picked up a rusty and dirty tin jagged at the edges from the tin-opener. It was a blue Wood, Dunn butter tin from Australia. Into that he poured the water for the girl. That was how Willie Chandran's mother learned that in the world outside aluminium was for Muslims and Christians and people of that sort, brass was for people of caste, and a rusty old tin was for her. She spat on the tin. The half-starved water man made as if to hit her with the bamboo dipper and she ran out of the schoolyard fearing for her life, with the man cursing her as she ran. After some weeks she began to go to the mission school. She should have gone there from the start, but her family and group knew nothing about anything. They didn't know about the religion of the people of caste or the Muslims or the Christians. They didn't know what was happening in the country or the world. They had lived in ignorance, cut off from the world, for centuries.

Willie's blood boiled whenever he heard the story about the Wood, Dunn butter tin. He loved his mother, and when he was very young he used such money as came his way to buy pretty things for her and the house: a bamboo-framed mirror, a bamboo wall-stand for a vase, a nice length of block-stamped cloth, a brass vase, a painted papier-mâché box from Kashmir, crêpe-paper flowers. But gradually as he grew up he understood more about the mission school and its position in the state. He understood more about the pupils in the school. He understood that to go to the mission school was to be branded, and he began to look at his mother from more and more of a distance. The more successful he became at school – and he was better than his fellows – the greater that distance grew.

He began to long to go to Canada, where his teachers came from. He even began to think he might adopt their religion and become like them and travel the world teaching. And one day, when he was asked to write an English 'composition' about his holidays he pretended he was a Canadian, with parents who were called 'Mom' and 'Pop'. Mom and Pop had one day decided to take the kids to the beach. They had gone upstairs early in the morning to the children's room to wake them up, and the children had put on their new holiday clothes and they had driven off in the family car to the beach. The beach was full of holidaymakers, and the family had eaten the holiday sweets they had brought with them and at the end of the day, tanned and content, they had driven home. All the details of this foreign life – the upstairs house, the children's room – had been taken from American comic books which had been circulating in the mission school. These details had been mixed up with local details, like the holiday clothes and the holiday sweets, some of which Mom and Pop had at one stage out of their own great content given to half-naked beggars. This composition was awarded full marks, ten out of ten, and Willie was asked to read it out to the class. The other boys, many of whom lived very poor lives, had had no idea what to write about, and had not even been able to invent, knowing nothing of the world. They listened with adoration to Willie's story. He took the exercise book and showed it to his mother, and she was pleased and proud. She said to Willie, 'Show it to your father. Literature was his subject.'

Willie didn't take the book directly to his father. He left it on the table in the verandah overlooking the inner ashram yard. His father had coffee there in the morning.

He read the composition. He was ashamed. He thought, 'Lies, lies. Where did he get these lies from?' Then he thought, 'But is it worse than Shelley and W and the rest of them? All of that was lies too.' He read the composition again. He grieved at his disappearance and thought, 'Little Willie, what have I done to you?' He finished his coffee. He heard the first of the day's suppliants assembling in the main courtyard of his little temple. He thought, 'But I have done him nothing. He is not me. He is his mother's son. All this Mom-and-Pop business comes from her. She can't help it. It's her background. She has these mission-school ambitions. Perhaps after a few hundred rebirths she will be more evolved. But she can't wait like other decent folk. Like so many backwards nowadays, she wants to jump the gun.'

He never mentioned the composition to Willie, and Willie never asked. He despised his father more than ever.

One morning a week or so later, while his father was with clients on the ashram side of the house, Willie Chandran again left his composition exercise book on the table in the verandah of the inner courtyard. His father saw the book at lunchtime, and became agitated. His first feeling was that there was another offensive composition in the book, more about Mom and Pop. He felt the boy, true son of his mother, was challenging him, with all the slyness of a backward, and he wasn't sure what he should do. He asked himself, 'What would the mahatma do?' He decided that the mahatma would have met this kind of sly aggression with his own kind of civil disobedience: he would have done nothing. So he did nothing. He didn't touch the exercise book. He left it where it was, and Willie saw it when he came back from school during the lunch hour.

Willie thought in his head, in English, 'He is not only a fraud, but a coward.' The sentence didn't sound right; there was a break in the logic somewhere. So he did it over. 'Not only is he a fraud, but he is also a coward.' The inversion in the beginning of the sentence worried him, and the 'but' seemed odd, and the 'also'. And then, on the way back to the Canadian mission school, the grammatical fussiness of his composition class took over. He tried out other versions of the sentence in his head, and he found when he got to the school that he had forgotten his father and the occasion.

But Willie Chandran's father hadn't forgotten Willie. The silence and smugness of the boy at lunchtime had disturbed him. He knew there was something treacherous in the exercise book, and then very quickly in the afternoon he became sure. He left a client in the middle of a foolish consultation and went to the verandah on the other side. He opened the exercise book and saw that week's composition. It was headed 'King Cophetua and the Beggar-maid'.

In a far-off time, when there was famine and general distress in the land, a beggar-maid, braving every kind of danger on the road, went to the court of the king, Cophetua, to ask for alms. She gained admittance to the king. Her head was covered, and she looked down at the ground and spoke so beautifully and with such modesty that the king begged her to uncover her head. She was of surpassing beauty. The king fell in love with her and swore a royal oath there and then, before his court, that the beggar-maid was going to be his queen. He was as good as his word. But his queen's happiness didn't last. No one treated her like a real queen; everyone knew she was a beggar. She lost touch with her family. Sometimes they appeared outside the palace gates and called for her, but she wasn't allowed to go to them. She began to be openly insulted by the king's family and by people in the court. Cophetua seemed not to notice, and his queen was too ashamed to tell him. In time Cophetua and his queen had a son. There were many more insults in the court after that, and curses from the queen's beggar relations. The son, growing up, suffered for his mother's sake. He made a vow to get even with them all, and when he became a man he carried out his vow: he killed Cophetua. Everybody was happy, the people in the court, the beggars at the palace gates.

There the story ended. All down the margin of the exercise book the red pen of the missionary teacher had ticked and ticked in approval.

Willie Chandran's father thought, 'We've created a monster. He really hates his mother and his mother's people, and she doesn't know. But his mother's uncle was the firebrand of the backwards. I mustn't forget that. The boy will poison what remains of my life. I must get him far away from here.'

One day not long after he said, in as gentle a way as he could (it wasn't easy for him to talk gently to this boy), 'We have to think of your higher education, Willie. You mustn't be like me.'

Willie said, 'Why do you say that? You are pretty pleased with what you do.'

His father didn't take up the provocation. He said, 'I responded to the mahatma's call. I burnt my English books in the front courtyard of the university.'

Willie Chandran's mother said, 'Not many people noticed.'

'You can say what you please. I burnt my English books and I didn't get a degree. All I'm saying now, if I'm allowed, is that Willie should get a degree.'

Willie said, 'I want to go to Canada.'

His father said, 'For me it's been a life of sacrifice. I have earned no fortune. I can send you to Benares or Bombay or Calcutta or even Delhi. But I can't send you to Canada.'

'The fathers will send me.'

'Your mother has put this low idea in your head. Why would the fathers want to send you to Canada?'

'They will make me a missionary.'

'They will turn you into a little monkey and send you right back here to work with your mother's family and the other backwards. You are a fool.'

Willie Chandran said, 'You think so?' And put an end to the discussion.

A few days later the exercise book was on the verandah table. Willie Chandran's father didn't hesitate. He flicked through the red-ticked pages to the last composition.

It was a story. It was the longest thing in the book and it looked as though it had been written at a great rate. The fast, small, pressing-down handwriting had crinkled every page, and the teacher with the red pen had liked it all, sometimes drawing a red vertical line in the margin and giving one tick to a whole paragraph or page.

The story was set, like Willie's other stories or fables, in an undefined place, at an undated time. It began at a time of famine. Even the brahmins were affected. A starving brahmin, all skin and bones, decides to leave his community and go elsewhere, into the hot rocky wilderness, to die alone, with dignity. Near the limit of his strength, he finds a low dark cavern in a cliff and decides to die there. He purifies himself as best he can and settles down to sleep for the last time. He rests his wasted head on a rock. Something about the rock irritates the brahmin's neck and head. He reaches back to touch the rock with his hand, once, twice, and then he knows that the rock isn't a rock. It is a hard grimy sack of some sort, full of ridges, and when the brahmin sits up he discovers that the rock is really a very old sack of treasure.

As soon as he makes the discovery a spirit calls out to him, 'This treasure has been waiting for you for centuries. It is yours to keep, and will be yours for ever, on condition that you do something for me. Do you accept?' The trembling brahmin says, 'What must I do for you?' The spirit says, 'Every year you must sacrifice a fresh young child to me. As long as you do that, the treasure will stay with you. If you fail, the treasure will vanish and return here. Over the centuries there have been many before you, and all have failed.' The brahmin doesn't know what to say. The spirit says with irritation, 'Dying man, do you accept?' The brahmin says, 'Where will I find the children?' The spirit says, 'It is not for me to give you help. If you are resolute enough you will find a way. Do you accept?' And the brahmin says, 'I accept.' The spirit says, 'Sleep, rich man. When you awaken you will be in your old temple and the world will be at your feet. But never forget your pledge.'

The brahmin awakens in his old home and finds himself well fed and sturdy. He also awakens to the knowledge that he is rich beyond the dreams of avarice. And almost immediately, before he can savour his joy, the thought of his pledge begins to torment him. The torment doesn't go away. It corrupts all his hours, all the minutes of all the hours.

One day he sees a group of tribal people passing in front of the temple compound. They are black and small, bony from starvation, and almost naked. Hunger has driven these people from their habitations and made them careless of old rules. They should not pass so close to the temple because the shadow of these people, their very sight, even the sound of their voices, is polluting. The brahmin has an illumination. He finds out where the tribal encampment is. He goes there at night with his face hidden by his shawl. He seeks out the headman and in the name of charity and religion he offers to buy one of the half-dead tribal children. He makes this deal with the tribal headman: the child is to be drugged and taken to a certain low cave in the rocky wilderness and left there. If this is fairly and honestly done, a week later the tribal man will find a piece of old treasure in the cave, enough to take all his followers out of their distress.

The sacrifice is done, the piece of old treasure laid down; and from year to year this ritual goes on, for the brahmin, and for the tribals.

One year the headman, now better fed and better dressed, with shiny oiled hair, comes to the brahmin's temple. The brahmin is rough. He says, 'Who are you?' The headman says, 'You know me. And I know you. I know what you are up to. I have known all along. I recognised you that first night and understood everything. I want half your treasure.' The brahmin says, 'You know nothing. I know that for fifteen years you and your tribe have been carrying out child-sacrifice in a certain cave. It is part of your tribal ways. Now you have all prospered and become townsmen you are ashamed and frightened. So you have come and confessed to me and asked for my understanding. I have given you that, because I understand your tribal ways, but I cannot say I am not horrified, and if I choose I can lead anyone to the cave with the bones of many children. Now get out. Your hair is oiled, but your very shadow pollutes this sacred place.' The headman cringes and backs away. He says, 'Forgive, forgive.' The brahmin says, 'And don't forget your pledge.'

The time comes for the brahmin's annual sacrifice. He makes his way at night to the cave of bones. He turns over and polishes every kind of story in case the tribal chief has informed on him and people are waiting for him. No one is waiting. He is not surprised. In the dark cave there are two drugged children. The headman has, after all, behaved well. With a practised hand the brahmin sacrifices the two to the spirit of the cave. When he comes to burn the little corpses he sees by the light of his wood torch that they are his own children.

This was where the story ended. Willie's father had read without skipping. And when, mechanically, he turned back to the beginning he saw – what he had forgotten during the reading – that the story was called 'A Life of Sacrifice'.

He thought, 'His mind is diseased. He hates me and he hates his mother, and now he's turned against himself. This is what the missionaries have done to him with Mom and Pop and Dick Tracy and the Justice Society of America comic magazine, and Christ on the Cross movies in Passion Week, and Bogart and Cagney and George Raft the rest of the time. I cannot deal rationally with this kind of hatred. I will deal with it in the way of the mahatma. I will ignore it. I will keep a vow of silence so far as he is concerned.'

Two or three weeks later the boy's mother came to him and said, 'I wish you would break that vow of silence. It is making Willie very unhappy.'

'The boy is lost. There is nothing I can do for him.'

She said, 'You have to help him. No one else can. Two days ago I found him sitting in the dark. When I put the light on I saw he was crying. I asked him why. He said, "I just feel that everything in the world is so sad. And it is all that we have. I don't know what to do." I didn't know what to say to him. It's something he gets from your side. I tried to comfort him. I told him that everything would be all right, and he would go to Canada. He said he didn't want to go to Canada. He didn't want to be a missionary. He didn't even want to go back to the school.'

'Something must have happened at the school.'

'I asked him. He said he went to the principal's office for something. There was a magazine on the table. It was a missionary magazine. There was a colour picture on the cover. A priest with glasses and a wristwatch was standing with one foot on a statue of the Buddha. He had just chopped it down with an axe, and he was smiling and leaning on the axe like a lumberjack. I used to see magazines and pictures like that when I was at the school. It didn't worry me. But when Willie saw the picture he felt ashamed for himself. He felt the fathers had been fooling him all these years. He was ashamed that he ever wanted to be a missionary. All he really wanted was to go to Canada and get away from here. Until he saw that picture he didn't know what missionary work was.'

'If he doesn't want to go to the mission school he doesn't have to go.'

'Like father, like son.'

'The mission school was your idea.'

So Willie Chandran stopped going to the mission school. He began to idle at home.

His father saw him one day asleep face down, a closed copy of a school edition of *The Vicar of Wakefield* beside him, his feet crossed, the red soles much lighter than the rest of him. There was such unhappiness and such energy there that he was overwhelmed with pity. He thought, 'I used to think that you were me and I was worried at what I had done to you. But now I know that you are not me. What is in my head is not in yours. You are somebody else, somebody I don't know, and I worry for you because you are launched on a journey I know nothing of.'

Some days later he sought out Willie and said, 'I have no fortune, as you know. But if you want, I will write to some of the people I know in England and we'll see what they can do for you.'

Willie was pleased but he didn't show it.

The famous writer after whom Willie was named was now very old. After some weeks a reply came from him from the south of France. The letter, on a small sheet of paper, was professionally typewritten, in narrow lines with a lot of clear space. *Dear Chandran, It was very nice getting your letter. I have nice memories of the country, and it is nice hearing from Indian friends. Yours very sincerely* ... There was nothing in the letter about Willie. It was as though the old writer hadn't understood what was being asked of him. There would have been secretaries. They would have stood in the way. But Willie Chandran's father was disappointed and ashamed. He resolved not to tell Willie, but Willie had a good idea of what had happened: he had seen the letter with the French stamp arrive.

There was no reply from a famous wartime broadcaster who had come out to India to cover independence and partition and the assassination of the mahatma, and had been exceptionally friendly. Some people who replied were direct. They said they couldn't do anything. Some sent long friendly replies that, like the writer's, ignored the request for help.

Willie's father tried to be philosophical, but it wasn't easy. He said to his wife – though it was his rule to keep his depressions to himself – 'I did so much for them when they came here. I gave them the run of the ashram. I introduced them to everybody.' His wife said, 'They did a lot for you too. They gave you your business. You can't deny it.' He thought, 'I will never talk to her about these matters again. I was wrong to break my rule. She is quite without shame. She is a backward through and through. Eating my salt and abusing me.'

He wondered how he would break the bad news to Willie. Now that he had understood the boy's weakness, he didn't worry about the scorn. But – still a little to his surprise – he didn't want to add to the boy's suffering. He couldn't forget the picture of the ambitious, defeated boy sleeping face down with the dead old school text of *The Vicar of Wakefield* beside him, his feet crossed, feet as dark as his mother's.

But he was spared the humiliation of an all-round refusal. There came a letter in a blue envelope from London, from the House of Lords, from a famous man who had paid a brief visit to the ashram just after independence. His fame and his title had made him memorable to Willie Chandran's father.

The First Chapter

The big and fluent handwriting on the blue House of Lords paper spoke of power and display, and what was in the letter matched the handwriting. It had pleased the great man to display his power to Willie's father, to win gratitude and merit in that far-off corner, to wave a wand, to lift a little finger, as it were (all the other fingers being busy about greater matters), and set many little men in motion. The letter contained a little of the gold the little men had spun: a place and a scholarship had been found for Willie Chandran in a college of education for mature students in London.

And that was how, when he was twenty, Willie Chandran, the mission-school student who had not completed his education, with no idea of what he wanted to do, except to get away from what he knew, and yet with very little idea of what lay outside what he knew, only with the fantasies of the Hollywood films of the thirties and forties that he had seen at the mission school, went to London.

* * *

HE WENT BY SHIP. And everything about the journey so frightened him – the size of his own country, the crowds in the port, the number of ships in the harbour, the confidence of the people on the ship – that he found himself unwilling to speak, at first out of pure worry, and then, when he discovered that silence brought him strength, out of policy. So he looked without trying to see and heard without listening; and yet later – just as after an illness it may be possible for someone to recall everything he had at the time only half noticed – he was to find that he had stored up all the details of that stupendous first crossing.

He knew that London was a great city. His idea of a great city was of a fairyland of splendour and dazzle, and when he got to London and began walking about its streets he felt let down. He didn't know what he was looking at. The little booklets and folders he picked up or bought at Underground stations didn't help; they assumed that the local sights they were writing about were famous and well understood; and really Willie knew little more of London than the name.

The only two places he knew about in the city were Buckingham Palace and Speakers' Corner. He was disappointed by Buckingham Palace. He thought the maharaja's palace in his own state was far grander, more like a palace, and this made him feel, in a small part of his heart, that the kings and queens of England were impostors, and the country a little bit of a sham. His disappointment turned to something like shame – at himself, for his gullibility – when he went to Speakers' Corner. He had heard of this place in the general knowledge class at the mission school and he had written knowingly about it in more than one end-of-term examination. He expected big, radical, shouting crowds, like those his mother's uncle, the firebrand of the backwards, used to address. He didn't expect to see an idle scatter of people around half a dozen talkers, with the big buses and the cars rolling indifferently by all the time. Some of the talkers had very personal religious ideas, and Willie, remembering his own home life, thought that the families of these men might have been glad to get them out of the house in the afternoons.

He turned away from the depressing scene and began

to walk down one of the paths beside Bayswater Road. He walked without seeing, thinking of the hopelessness of home and his own nebulous present. All at once, in the most magical way, he was lifted out of himself. He saw, walking towards him on the path, half leaning on the stick he carried, a man famous beyond imagining, and now casual and solitary and grand among the afternoon strollers. Willie looked hard. All kinds of old attitudes awakened in him – the very attitudes of some of the people who came to the ashram just to gaze on his father – and he felt ennobled by the sight and presence of the great man.

The man was tall and slender, very dark and striking, in a formal charcoal double-breasted suit that emphasised his slenderness. His crinkly hair was combed back flat above a long, narrow face with an amazing hawk-like nose. Every detail of the man approaching him answered the photographs Willie knew. It was Krishna Menon, the close friend of Mr Nehru, and India's spokesman in international forums. He was looking down as he walked, preoccupied. He looked up, saw Willie, and out of a clouded face flashed him a friendly satanic smile. Willie had never expected to be acknowledged by the great man. And then, before he could work out what to do, he and Krishna Menon had crossed, and the dazzling moment was over.

A day or so later, in the little common room of the college, he saw in a newspaper that Krishna Menon had passed through London on his way to New York and the United Nations. He had stayed at Claridge's hotel. Willie looked at maps and directories and worked out that Krishna Menon might simply have walked that afternoon from the hotel to the park, to think about the speech he was soon going to make. The speech was to be about the invasion of Egypt by Britain and France and others.

Willie knew nothing about that invasion. The invasion had apparently been caused by the nationalisation of the Suez Canal, and Willie knew nothing about that either. He knew, from his school geography lessons, about the Suez Canal; and one of the Hollywood movies they had shown at the mission school was *Suez*. But in Willie's mind neither his school geography nor *Suez* was strictly real. Neither had to do with the here and now; neither affected him or his family or his town; and he had no idea of the history of the canal or Egypt. He knew the name of Colonel Nasser, the Egyptian leader, but it was only in the way he knew about Krishna Menon: he knew about the greatness of the man without knowing about the deeds. At home he had read the newspapers, but he read them in his own way. He had learned to shut out the main stories, the ones about far-off wars or election campaigns in the United States that meant nothing to him and went on week after week and were slow and repetitive and then ended, very often quite lamely, giving, like a bad book or movie, nothing or very little for much effort and attention. So, just as on the ship Willie was able to watch without seeing and hear without listening, Willie at home for many years read the newspapers without taking in the news. He knew the big names; very occasionally he looked at the main headline; but that was all.

Now, after his sight of Krishna Menon in the park, he was amazed at how little he knew of the world around him. He said, 'This habit of non-seeing I have got from my father.'

He began to read about the Egyptian crisis in the newspapers, but he didn't understand what he read. He knew too little about the background, and newspaper stories were like serials; it was necessary to know what had gone before. So he began to read about Egypt in the college library, and he floundered. It was like moving very fast and having no fixed markers to give an idea of position and speed. His ignorance seemed to widen with everything he read. He turned in the end to a cheap history of the world published during the war. This he could hardly understand. It was as with the leaflets about London in the Underground stations: the book assumed that the reader already knew about famous events. Willie thought he was swimming in ignorance, had lived without a knowledge of time. He remembered one of the things his mother's uncle used to say: that the backwards had been shut out for so long from society that they knew nothing of India, nothing of the other religions, nothing even of the religion of the people of caste, whose serfs they were. And he thought, 'This blankness is one of the things I have got from my mother's side.'

His father had given him names of people he should get in touch with. Willie hadn't intended to do so. Very few of the names meant anything to him, and he wished, in London, to steer clear of his father, and to get by on his own. That didn't prevent him boasting of the names in the college. He dropped the names in an innocent, trying-out way, gauging the weight of each name from the way people reacted to it. And now, out of his new feeling of ignorance and shame, his developing vision of a world too big for him, Willie wrote to the famous old writer after whom he had been named and to a journalist whose name he had seen in big letters in one of the newspapers.

The journalist replied first. *Dear Chandran, Of course I remember your father. My favourite babu . . .* 'Babu', an anglicised Indian, was a mistake; the word should have been 'sadhu', an ascetic. But Willie didn't mind. The letter seemed friendly. It asked Willie to come to the newspaper office, and early one afternoon a week or so later Willie made his way to Fleet Street. It was warm and bright, but Willie had been made to believe that it rained all the time in England, and he wore a raincoat. The raincoat was very thin, of a rubbery material that sweated on the very smooth inside almost as soon as it was worn; so that by the time Willie had got to the big black newspaper building the top and sides of his jacket and the back of his collar were damp, and when he took off the sweated, clinging raincoat he looked as though he had walked through a drizzle.

He gave his name to a man in uniform, and after a while the journalist, in a dark suit and not young, came down and he and Willie talked standing up in the lobby. They didn't get on. They didn't have anything to talk about. The journalist asked about the babu; Willie didn't correct him; and when they had finished that subject they both looked about them. The journalist began to talk about the newspaper in a defensive way, and Willie understood that the newspaper didn't like Indian independence and was not friendly to India and that the journalist himself had written some hard pieces after his visit to the country.

The journalist said, 'It's Beaverbrook, really. He has no time for Indians. He's like Churchill in some respects.'

Willie said, 'Who is Beaverbrook?'

The journalist dropped his voice. 'He's our proprietor.' It amused him that Willie didn't know something so stupendous.

Willie noticed, and thought, 'I am glad I didn't know. I am glad I wasn't impressed.'

Somebody had come through the main door, which was at Willie's back. The journalist looked to one side of Willie, to follow the progress of the new arrival.

He said, with awe, 'That's our editor.'

Willie saw a dark-suited middle-aged man, pink-faced after lunch, going up the steps at the far side of the lobby.

The journalist, gazing at his editor, said, 'His name is Arthur Christiansen. They say he is the greatest editor in the world.' Then, as though speaking to himself, he said, 'It takes a lot to get there.' Willie looked with the journalist at the great man going up the steps. Then, setting aside that mood, the journalist said in a jokey way, 'I hope you haven't come to ask for his job.'

Willie didn't laugh. He said, 'I'm a student. I am here on a scholarship. I am not looking for a job.'

'Where are you?'

Willie gave the name of his college.

The journalist didn't know it. Willie thought, 'He's trying to insult me. My college is quite big and quite real.'

The journalist said in his new jokey way, 'Are you asthmatic? I ask only because our proprietor is asthmatic and he has a special feeling for asthmatics. If you wanted a job it would be something in your favour.'

That was where the meeting ended, and Willie was ashamed for his father, who must have been mocked by the journalist in what he wrote, and ashamed at himself for having gone back on his decision to stay away from his father's friends.

A few days later there came a letter from the great writer after whom Willie was named. It was on a small sheet of Claridge's paper – the very hotel from where Krishna Menon had set out on his short walk to the park that afternoon, no doubt to think about his United Nations speech about Suez. The letter was typewritten, double-spaced and with wide margins. *Dear Willie Chandran, It was nice getting your letter. I have very nice memories of India, and it is always nice hearing from Indian friends. Yours very sincerely* ... And the shaky, old man's signature was yet carefully done, as though the writer felt that was the point of his letter.

Willie thought, 'I misjudged my father. I used to think that the world was easy for him as a brahmin and that he became a fraud out of idleness. Now I begin to understand how hard the world must have been for him.'

Willie was living in the college as in a daze. The learning he was being given was like the food he was eating, without savour. The two were inseparable in his mind. And just as he ate without pleasure, so, with a kind of blindness, he did what the lecturers and tutors asked of him, read the books and articles and did the essays. He was unanchored, with no idea of what lay ahead. He still had no idea of the scale of things, no idea of historical time or even of distance. When he had seen Buckingham Palace he had thought that the kings and queens were impostors, and the country a sham, and he continued to live within that idea of make-believe.

At the college he had to re-learn everything that he knew.

He had to learn how to eat in public. He had to learn how to greet people and how, having greeted them, not to greet them all over again in a public place ten or fifteen minutes later. He had to learn to close doors behind him. He had to learn how to ask for things without being peremptory.

The college was a semi-charitable Victorian foundation and it was modelled on Oxford and Cambridge. That was what the students were often told. And because the college was like Oxford and Cambridge it was full of various pieces of 'tradition' that the teachers and students were proud of but couldn't explain. There were rules, for instance, about dress and behaviour in the dining hall; and there were quaint, beer-drinking punishments for misdemeanours. Students had to wear black gowns on formal occasions. When Willie asked about the gowns, he was told by one of the lecturers that it was what was done at Oxford and Cambridge, and that the academic gown was descended from the ancient Roman toga. Willie, not knowing enough to be awed, and following mission-school ways, looked up the matter in various books in the college library. He read that, in spite of all the toga-clad statues from the ancient world, no one had so far been able to work out how the old Romans put on their togas. The academic gown probably was copied from the Islamic seminaries of a thousand years before, and that Islamic style would have been copied from something earlier. So it was a piece of make-believe.

Yet something strange was happening. Gradually, learning the quaint rules of his college, with the churchy Victorian buildings pretending to be older than they were, Willie began to see in a new way the rules he had left behind at home. He began to see – and it was upsetting, at first – that the old rules were themselves a kind of make-believe, self-imposed. And one day, towards the end of his second term, he saw with great clarity that the old rules no longer bound him.

His mother's firebrand uncle had agitated for years for freedom for the backwards. Willie had always put himself on that side. Now he saw that the freedom the firebrand had been agitating about was his for the asking. No one he met, in the college or outside it, knew the rules of Willie's own place, and Willie began to understand that he was free to present himself as he wished. He could, as it were, write his own revolution. The possibilities were dizzying. He could, within reason, re-make himself and his past and his ancestry.

And just as in the college he had boasted in the beginning in an innocent, lonely way of the friendship of his 'family' with the famous old writer and the famous Beaverbrook journalist, so now he began to alter other things about himself, but in small, comfortable ways. He had no big over-riding idea. He took a point here and another there. The newspapers, for instance, were full of news about the trade unions, and it occurred to Willie one day that his mother's uncle, the fire-brand of the backwards, who sometimes at public meetings wore a red scarf (in imitation of his hero, the famous backward revolutionary and atheistic poet Bharatidarsana), it occurred to Willie that this uncle of his mother's was a kind of trade-union leader, a pioneer of workers' rights. He let drop the fact in conversation and in tutorials, and he noticed that it cowed people.

It occurred to him at another time that his mother, with her mission-school education, was probably half a Christian.

He began to speak of her as a full Christian; but then, to get rid of the mission-school taint and the idea of laughing bare-foot backwards (the college supported a Christian mission in Nyasaland in Southern Africa, and there were mission maga-zines in the common room), he adapted certain things he had read, and he spoke of his mother as belonging to an ancient Christian community of the subcontinent, a community almost as old as Christianity itself. He kept his father as a brahmin. He made his father's father a 'courtier'. So, playing with words, he began to re-make himself. It excited him, and began to give him a feeling of power.

His tutors said, 'You seem to be settling in.'

* * *

HIS NEW CONFIDENCE began to draw people to him. One of them was Percy Cato. Percy was a Jamaican of mixed parentage and was more brown than black. Willie and Percy, both exotics, both on scholarships, had been wary of one another in the beginning, but now they met easily and began to exchange stories of their antecedents. Percy, explaining his ancestry, said, 'I think I even have an Indian grandmother.' And Willie, below his new shell, felt a pang. He thought that woman might have been like his mother, but in an impossibly remote setting, where the world would have been altogether outside her control. Percy put his hand on his crinkly hair and said, 'The Negro is actually recessive.' Willie didn't understand what Percy meant. He knew only that Percy had worked out a story to explain his own appearance. He was a Jamaican but not strictly of Jamaica. He was born in Panama and had grown up there. He said, 'I am the only black man or Jamaican or West Indian you'll meet in England who knows nothing about cricket.'

Willie said, 'How did you get to Panama?'

'My father went to work on the Panama Canal.'

'Like the Suez Canal?' It was still in the news.

'This was before the First War.'

In his mission-school way Willie looked up the Panama Canal in the college library. And there it all was, in grainy, touched-up, imprecise, black-bordered photographs in old encyclopaedias and annuals: the great, waterless engineering works before the First War, with gangs of faceless black workers, possibly Jamaicans, in the waterless locks. One of those black men might have been Percy's father.

He asked Percy in the common room, 'What did your father do in the Panama Canal?'

'He was a clerk. You know those people over there. They can't read and write at all.'

Willie thought, 'He's lying. That's a foolish story. His father went there as a labourer. He would have been in one of the gangs, holding his pickaxe before him on the ground, like the others, and looking obediently at the photographer.'

Until then Willie hadn't really known what to make of a man who appeared to have no proper place in the world and could be both Negro and not Negro in his ways. When Percy was in his Negro mode he claimed fellowship with Willie; in the other mode he wanted to keep Willie at a distance. Now, with that picture in his head of Percy's father standing, like a soldier at ease, with both hands on the haft of his pickaxe in the hot Panama sun, Willie felt he knew him a little better.

Willie had been very careful with what he had told Percy about himself, and it was easier now for him to be with Percy. He felt he stood a rung or two or many rungs above Percy, and he was more willing to acknowledge Percy as the man about town, the man who knew more about London and western ways. Percy was flattered, and he became Willie's guide to the city.

Percy loved clothes. He always wore a suit and a tie. His shirt-collars were always clean and starched and stiff, and his shoes were always polished, with new-looking insteps and heels that were nice and solid and never worn down. Percy knew about cloth and the cut of suits and handstitching, and he could spot these things on people as he walked. Good clothes seemed, almost, to have a moral quality for him; he respected people who respected clothes.

Willie knew nothing about clothes. He had five white shirts and – since the college laundry went off once a week – he had to keep one shirt going for two or three days. He had one tie, a burgundy-coloured Tootal cotton tie that cost six shillings. Every three months he bought a new one and threw away the old one, dreadfully stained and too wrinkled to knot. He had one jacket, a light-green thing that didn't absolutely fit and couldn't hold a shape. He had paid three pounds for it at a sale of The Fifty Shilling Tailors in the Strand. He didn't think of himself as badly dressed, and it was some time before he noticed that Percy was particular about clothes and liked to talk about them. He used to wonder about this taste of Percy's. A fussiness about cloth and colour was something he associated with women (and in a now secret part of his mind he thought of the backwards on his mother's side, and their love of strong colour). It was wrong and effeminate and idle in a man. But now he thought he understood why Percy loved clothes and, more than clothes, shoes. And then he found he was wrong about the effeminacy.

Percy said one day, 'My girlfriend is coming this Saturday.' Women were allowed in the students' rooms on weekends. 'I don't know whether you have noticed, Willie, but on weekends the college rocks with fuck.'

Willie was full of excitement and jealousy, especially because of the blunt and easy way Percy had spoken. He said, 'I would like to meet your girlfriend.'

Percy said, 'Come and have a drink on Saturday.'

And Willie could hardly wait for Saturday.

A little while later he asked Percy, 'What is the name of your girlfriend?'

Percy said, with surprise, 'June.'

The name was fragrant for Willie. And later, during the same conversation, he asked as casually as he could, 'What does June do?'

'She works at the perfume counter in Debenhams.'

Perfume counter, Debenhams: the words intoxicated Willie. Percy noticed and, wishing to add to his grand London effect, said, 'Debenhams is a big store in Oxford Street.'

After a while Willie asked, 'Was that where you met June? At the perfume counter in Debenhams?'

'I met her at the club.'

'Club!'

'A drinking place where I used to work.'

Willie was shocked, but he thought he should hide it. He said, 'Of course.'

Percy said, 'I worked there before coming here. It was owned by a friend of mine. I can take you if you want.'

They went by Underground to Marble Arch. That was where, many months before, Willie had got off to go to look for Speakers' Corner, and had had the adventure of seeing Krishna Menon. It was quite another London Willie had in mind when he and Percy made for a quiet narrow street north of Oxford Street at the back of a big hotel. The club, announced by the smallest of signs, was a small, shut-in, very dark room off a lobby. A black man was behind the counter, and a woman with pale hair and pale, over-powdered skin and a pale dress was sitting on a stool. They both greeted Percy. Willie was stirred, not by the beauty of the woman – she had little of that, and seemed to get older the more he looked at her – but by her coarseness, her tawdriness, by her being there in the afternoon, by her having prepared so carefully for being there, and by the very strong idea of vice. Percy ordered whisky for both of them, though neither he nor Willie was a drinker; and they sat and didn't drink, and Percy talked.

Percy said, 'I was the front-of-house man here, being smooth with the smooth and rough with the rough. It was all I could get. In a place like London a man like me has to take what he can get. I thought one day I should ask for a piece of the business. My friend cut up rough. I thought I should leave, to save the friendship. My friend's a dangerous man. You'll meet him. I'll introduce you.'

Willie said, 'And June came here one day, from the perfume counter at Debenhams?'

'It's not far away. It's an easy walk.'

Willie, though not knowing what June was like, and where Debenhams was, tried many times to recreate in his mind that walk from Debenhams to the club.

He saw her on Saturday in Percy's room at the college. She was a big girl in a tight skirt that showed off her hips. She filled the small room with her perfume. At her counter, Willie thought, she would have access to all the perfumes in Debenhams, and she had been lavish. Willie had never known perfume like that, that mingled smell of excrement and sweat and deep, piercing, many-sided sweetness from no simple source.

They were sitting together on the small college sofa and he allowed himself to press against her, more and more, while he took in her perfume, her plucked eyebrows, the depilated but slightly bristly legs she had drawn up below her.

Percy noticed but said nothing. Willie took that as the act of a friend. And June herself was gentle and yielding, even with Percy looking on. Willie had read that gentleness and softness in her face. When the time came for him to leave June and Percy to what they had to do, he was in a state. He thought he should look for a prostitute. He knew nothing about prostitutes, but he knew the reputation of some of the streets near Piccadilly Circus. But he didn't in the end have the courage.

On Monday he went to Debenhams. The girls at the perfume counter took fright at him, and he took fright at them, powdered, unreal, with strange lashes, and looking plucked and shaved like shop chickens. But he eventually found June. In this setting of glass and glitter and artificial light – an extraordinary London, such as he had looked for in the streets when he had just arrived – she was tall and soft and coarse and quite luscious. He could scarcely bear to consider all that had stirred him on Saturday. Below black-line eyebrows and mother-of-pearl eyelids her long eyelashes swept upwards. She greeted him without surprise. He was relieved, and even before he had spoken half a dozen words he saw that she understood his need and was going to be gentle with him. Even then, he found he didn't know how to press the matter, what words to use. All he could say was, 'Would you like to see me, June?'

She said, very simply, 'Of course, Willie.'

'Can we meet today? When you finish work.'

'Where should we meet?'

'The club.'

'Percy's old place? You have to be a member, you know.'

In the afternoon he went to the club, to see whether he could join. There was no trouble. Again, puzzlingly, there was no one there, apart from the very white woman on the stool and the black barman. The barman (who was perhaps in these quiet periods doing the job Percy did in the old days, being smooth with the smooth and rough with the rough) made Willie fill in a form. Willie then paid five pounds (he was living on seven pounds a week), and the barman – making little circles with his pen before he began to write, like a weight-lifter making feints at a mighty weight on the floor before he actually lifted – took a little time to write out Willie's name on a small membership card.

He watched the street for many minutes before the

appointed time, not wishing to be at the club first and then perhaps to be disappointed, and while he watched he played with pictures of June at the end of her working day getting ready somewhere and making her way from Debenhams to the club. He greeted her in the doorway when she came and they went inside, into the dark bar. The barman knew her, and the woman on the stool knew her, and Willie was pleased to be there with someone known. He bought drinks, expensive, fifteen shillings for the two, and all the while in the dark room he was smelling June's perfume and pressing against her and not paying attention to what he was saying.

She said, 'We can't go to the college. Percy wouldn't like it, and I can go there only on weekends.' A little later she said, 'All right. We'll go to the other place. We'll have to take a taxi.'

The driver made a face when she gave the address. The taxi took them away from the enchanted area of Marble Arch and Bayswater. It then turned north and very soon they were in wretched streets: big unkempt houses, without rails or fences, dustbins outside front windows. They stopped outside one such house. With the tip the fare was five shillings.

At the top of a rail-less flight of steps, a big, beaten-up door, with layers of old paint showing through in many places, led to a wide, dark hall smelling of old dirt, still with gas brackets on the walls. The wallpaper was almost black at the top; the linoleum on the floor ground down to no colour, though with pieces of the original pattern still at the edges. The stairs at the end of the hall were wide – old style there – but the wooden banisters were rough with grime. The landing window was unwashed and cracked, and the ground at the back was full of rubbish.

June said, 'It isn't the Ritz, but the natives are friendly.'

Willie wasn't so sure. Most of the doors were closed. But here and there, as they climbed – the steps narrowing – doors half opened and Willie saw the scowling, lined, yellow faces of very old women. So close to Marble Arch, but it was like another city, as though another sun shone on the college, as though another earth lay below the perfume counter at Debenhams.

The room June opened was small, with a mattress resting on newspapers on the bare floorboards. There was a chair and a towel and a naked hanging light bulb and not much else. June undressed methodically. It was too much for Willie. He hardly enjoyed the moment. In no time at all it was over for him, after a whole weekend of planning, after all the expense, and he didn't know what to say.

June, letting his head rest on her plump arm, said, 'A friend of mine says it happens with Indians. It's because of the arranged marriages. They don't feel they have to try hard. My father said his father used to tell him, 'Satisfy the woman first. Then think of yourself.' I don't suppose you had anybody telling you anything like that.'

Willie thought of his father with compassion for the first time.

He said, 'Let me try again, June.'

He tried again. It lasted longer, but June didn't say anything. And then, as before, the moment was over. The toilet was at the end of the black corridor. Spiderwebs, furry with dust, covered the high, rusting cistern, and hung like a kind of material on the small window at the top. June, when she came back, dressed very carefully. Willie didn't watch her. They walked down the steps without talking. A door opened and an old woman looked hard at them. An hour ago Willie would have minded; he didn't mind now. On a landing they saw a small black man with a broad-brimmed Jamaican hat that shadowed his face. His trousers, half of a zoot-suit, tight at the ankles and ballooning all down his legs, were in a thin material meant for a warmer place. He looked at them for longer than he should. They walked down the poor streets, which were very quiet, with big windows blank with sagging curtains and makeshift blinds, to where there was the light of shops and reasonable traffic, London again. No taxi for them now. A bus for June — she talked of going to Marble Arch to get a bus to a place called Cricklewood. Another bus for Willie. Going back to the college, thinking of June going home, to some place he couldn't imagine, thinking of Percy, he felt the beginning of remorse. It didn't last. He kicked it aside. He found he was pleased with himself, after all. He had done a good, an immense, afternoon's work. He was a changed man. He would worry about the money side later.

When he next saw Percy he asked, 'What's June's family like?'

'I don't know. I've never seen them. I don't think she likes them.'

Later he went to the college library and looked at a Pelican paperback, *The Physiology of Sex*. He had seen it around, but had been put off by the scientific title. The little wartime paperback was so tightly bound, with rusting metal staples, that it was hard sometimes to see the beginnings of lines. He had to pull at the pages and hold the book at different angles. He came at last to what he was looking for. He read that the average man could keep going for ten to fifteen minutes. That was bad news. A line or two later it became much worse. He read that a 'sexual athlete' could easily keep going for half an hour. The frivolous, gloating language – not something he expected in a serious Pelican book – was like a blow. He rejected what he had read, and read no more.

When he next saw Percy he asked, 'How did you learn about sex, Percy?'

Percy said, 'You have to start small. We all started small. Practising on the little girls. Don't look so shocked, little Willie. I am sure you don't know everything that was happening in your extended family. Your trouble, Willie, is that you are too neat. People look at you and don't see you.'

'You are neater than me. Always in a suit and a nice shirt.'

'I make women nervous. They are frightened of me. That's the way for you, Willie. Sex is a brutal business. You have to be brutal.'

'Is June frightened of you?'

'She is scared stiff of me. Ask her.'

Willie thought he should tell Percy about what had happened. But he didn't know what words to use. Something from an old movie came to him, and he was on the point of saying, 'June and I are in love, Percy.' But he didn't like the words, and they refused to come out.

Just a week or so later he was glad he hadn't said anything. Percy – the man about town – took him to a party in Notting Hill one Saturday evening. Willie knew nobody there and he stuck to Percy. June came in after a while. And a little while after that Percy said to Willie, 'This party is dull like hell. June and I are going back to the college to fuck.'

Willie looked at June and said, 'Is that true?'

She said in her simple way, 'Yes, Willie.'

If anybody had asked him, Willie would have said that Percy was teaching him about English life. In fact, through Percy, and without knowing what he was being introduced to, Willie was becoming part of the special, passing bohemian-immigrant life of London of the late 1950s. This hardly touched the traditional bohemian world of Soho. It was a little world on its own. The immigrants, from the Caribbean, and then the white colonies of Africa, and then Asia, had just arrived. They were still new and exotic; and there were English people – both high and low, with a taste for social adventure, a wish from time to time to break out of England, and people with colonial connections who wished in London to invert the social code of the colonies – there were English people who were ready to seek out the more stylish and approachable of the new arrivals. They met in Notting Hill, neutral territory, in dimly lit furnished flats in certain socially mixed squares (not far from where Willie and June had gone that evening); and they were gay and bright together. But few of the immigrants had proper jobs, or secure houses to go back to. Some of them were truly on the brink, and that gave an edge to the gaiety.

There was one man who frightened Willie. He was small and slender and handsome. He was white, or looked white. He said he came from the colonies and he had a kind of accent. From a distance he looked impeccable; close to, he was less impressive, the shirt dirty at the collar, the jacket worn, his skin oily, his teeth black and bad, his breath high. The first time he met Willie he told him his story. He came of a good colonial family, and had been sent by his father to London before the war, to be educated and to be groomed for English society. He had an English tutor. The tutor asked him one day, as part of his training, 'If you were going out to dinner and had the choice, would you go to the Ritz or the Berkeley?' The young man from the colonies said, 'The Ritz.' The tutor shook his head and said, 'Wrong. But a common error. The food at the Berkeley is better. Never forget it.' After the war there was a family quarrel and all that life ended. He had written or was writing about it, and he wanted to read a part of a chapter to Willie. Willie went to his room, in a boarding house not far away. He listened to an account of a visit to a psychiatrist. Very little of what was said by the psychiatrist was in the chapter. There was a lot about the view through the window, and about the antics of a cat on a fence. As Willie listened he felt that the psychiatrist's room was like the room where they were. And when at the end the writer asked Willie for his opinion Willie said, 'I wanted to know more about the patient and more about the doctor.' The writer went wild. His black eyes flashed, he showed his small tobacco-blackened teeth, and he shouted at Willie, 'I don't know who you are or where you come from or what talent you think you have. But a very famous person has said that I have added a new dimension to writing.' Willie ran out of the room, the man raging at him. But when they met again the man was easy. He said, 'Forgive me, old boy. It's that room. I hate it. I feel it's a coffin. Not what I was used to in the old days. I am moving.

Please forgive me. Please come and help me move. To show that you bear me no malice.' Willie went to the boarding house and knocked on the writer's door. A middle-aged woman came from a side door and said, 'So it's you. When he left yesterday he said he was sending somebody for his luggage. You can take his suitcase. But you must pay my back rent. I'll show you the book. Twenty weeks owing. It comes to sixty-six pounds and fifteen shillings.' Willie ran away again. Now when he went to Percy's parties he looked for the little man with the beard. It wasn't long before he saw him, and the man came up to him, sipping white wine from a wine glass, and said, his breath smelling of garlic and sausage, 'Sorry, old boy. But in South Africa we always said that you Indians were loaded, and I thought you would want to help.'

There appeared one evening a man unlike the usual bohemian partygoer. He brought a bottle of champagne for the party, and he presented it to Percy at the door. He was in his fifties, small, and carefully dressed in a grey suit with a check pattern, dressed almost to Percy's standards, with the lapels of the jacket handstitched, and the material falling soft over the arm. Percy introduced the stranger to Willie and left the two of them together.

Willie, not a drinking man, but knowing now what was expected of him, said, 'Champagne.'

The stranger said, in an extraordinarily soft voice, and an accent that was not the accent of a professional man, 'It's chilled. It's from the Ritz. They always keep a bottle ready for me.'

Willie wasn't sure that the man was serious. But the man's

eyes were cold and still, and Willie thought that it wasn't necessary for him to decide on the matter. But the Ritz again! How it seemed to matter to them. And to Willie – for whom at home a hotel was the cheapest kind of cheap tea-shop or eating place – it was a strange London idea of luxury: not the drink, not the treat, but the grand hotel, as though the extra price added an extra blessing.

The stranger wasn't going to make conversation with Willie, and Willie saw that he had to do some work.

He said, 'Do you work in London?'

The stranger said, 'I work right here. I'm a developer. I'm developing this area. It's a rubbish dump now. It will be different in twenty years. I'm willing to wait. There are all these protected old tenants, and they are paying nothing for their accommodation in these big houses, and they're almost in the centre of London. And they really want to live outside. In the leafy suburbs, or in a nice little country cottage. I help them do that. I buy the properties and offer the tenants other accommodation. Some take it. Some don't. Then I break up the place around them. In the old days I would get Percy to send in his darkies.' He spoke gently, without malice, purely descriptively, and Willie believed him.

Willie said, 'Percy?'

'Old London landlord. You didn't know? He didn't tell you?'

Percy said later that evening to Willie, 'So the old man cornered you.'

'He said you were a landlord.'

'I've had to do lots of things, little Willie. They wanted West Indian chaps to drive the buses here. But there was the problem of accommodation. People don't want to rent to black people. I don't have to tell you that. So one or two of the island governments encouraged people like me to buy properties and rent to West Indians. That was how it started. Don't get any fancy ideas. The houses I bought were full of people and cost about fifteen hundred pounds. One cost seventeen hundred and fifty. I used to fit in the boys in the spare rooms. I would go around every Friday evening to collect the rent. You couldn't get better people than the boys from Barbados. They were very grateful. On those Friday evenings, just off the London Transport shift, you would find every man Jack of them washed and clean and kneeling down beside the bed in their little rooms and praying. Bible on one side, open at Leviticus, rent book on the other side, closed over the notes. And the notes showing. The old man heard about me and decided to buy me out. I couldn't deny him. It was his manor. He offered me the job in the club. He promised me a piece of the business. When I asked for the piece he said I was being boring. I took the hint and got the college scholarship. But he wants to be friends with me still, and it is better for me to be friends with him. But it worries me, Willie. He wants me to go back to work for him. It worries me.'

Willie thought, 'How strange the city is! When I came to look for Speakers' Corner and saw Krishna Menon walking and thinking out his speech about the Suez invasion, I never knew that the club and Debenhams perfume counter were so close on one side, and Percy's old manor, and the old man's, so close on the other side.'

* * *

The First Chapter

IT WAS AT ONE OF those bohemian parties that Willie met a fattish young man with a beard who said he worked for the BBC. He edited or produced programmes for some of the overseas services. He was new in his job, and though personally modest, was full of the importance of what he did. He was a bureaucrat at heart, honouring convention, but in tribute to his job he felt he should put on bohemian airs in a place like Notting Hill, and extend patronage to people like Willie: lifting unlikely people up from the darkness to the glory of the airwaves.

He said to Willie, 'You have become more and more interesting to me as the minutes have ticked by.'

Willie had been working hard at his family history.

The producer said, 'Over here we don't know much about your kind of Christian community. So old, so early. So isolated from the rest of India, from what you say. It would be fascinating to hear about it. Why don't you do a script about it for us? It would fit nicely into one of our Commonwealth programmes. Five minutes. Six hundred and fifty words. Think of it as a page and a half of a Penguin book. No polemics. Five guineas if we use it.'

No one – leaving aside the scholarship people – had ever offered money to Willie before. And, almost as soon as the idea, and the angle, had been given to him by the producer, the five-minute talk had sketched itself in his mind. The beginnings of the faith in the subcontinent rendered as family stories (he would have to check things up in the encyclopaedia); the feeling of separateness from the rest of India; no true knowledge of the other religions of India; the family's work, in the British time, as social reformers, people

of Christian conscience, champions of workers' rights (a story
or two about the firebrand relation who wore a red scarf
when he addressed public meetings); the writer's education at
a mission school, and his discovery there of the tension
between the old Christian community and the new Christians,
backwards, recent converts, depressed people, full of griev-
ances; a difficult experience for the writer but in the end a
rewarding one, leading to an understanding and acceptance
not only of the new Christians, but also of the larger Indian
world outside the Christian fold, the Indian world from which
his ancestors had held aloof.

He wrote the talk in less than two hours. It was like being
at the mission school again: he knew what was expected of
him. A week later he had a letter of acceptance from the
producer, on a small, light sheet of BBC paper. The producer's
signature was very small. He was like a man happy to sink
his own identity in the grander identity of his corporation.
About three weeks later Willie was called to record his script.
He took the Underground to Holborn and walked down
Kingsway to Bush House. For the first time, doing that long
walk, with Bush House at the end of the mighty vista, he
had a sense of the power and wealth of London. It was
something he had looked for when he arrived but hadn't
found, and then, moving between his college and Notting
Hill, he had forgotten about.

He loved the drama of the studio, the red light and the
green light, the producer and the studio manager in their
sound-proof cubicle. His script was part of a longer magazine
programme. It was being recorded on disc, and he and the
other contributors had to sit through the whole thing twice.

The producer was fussy and full of advice for everybody. Willie listened carefully and picked up everything. Don't listen to your own voice; try to see what you are talking about; speak from the back of the throat; don't let your voice fall away at the end of a sentence. At the end the producer said to Willie, 'You're a natural.'

Four weeks later he was asked to go to an exhibition of carving by a young West African. The carver, a small man in embroidered, dirty-looking African cap and gown, was the only person in the gallery when Willie went. Willie was nervous at pretending to be a reporter, but the African talked easily. He said that when he looked at a piece of wood he saw the figures he was going to carve in it. He walked Willie round the exhibition, the heavy African gown bouncing off his thighs, and told him with great precision how much he had paid for every piece of wood. Willie built his script around that.

Two weeks later the producer sent him to a literary luncheon for an American hostess and gossip-writer. Her talk was about how to arrange a dinner party and how to deal with the problem of bores. Bores had to be put with other bores, the hostess said; fire had to be fought with fire. Willie's script wrote itself.

He found himself a little bit in demand. After recording a script one afternoon he bought a typewriter on hire-purchase from a firm in Southampton Row. He signed a long agreement for the twenty-four pounds' loan and (like Percy's West Indian lodgers with their rent books) he was given a little account book (with stiff covers, as though for long use) in which his payments were to be entered week by week.

He wrote more easily on the typewriter. He began to understand that a radio talk wasn't to be overloaded. He got to know just how much material was needed for a five-minute piece – three or four points were usually enough – and he didn't waste time looking for material he wasn't going to use. He got to know producers, studio managers, contributors. Some of the contributors were professionals. They lived in the suburbs and came in by train with big briefcases that held many little scripts for other programmes and outlines for other little scripts. They were busy people, planning little scripts for weeks and months ahead, and they didn't like sitting through a half-hour magazine programme twice. They looked bored by other people's pieces, and Willie learned to look bored by theirs.

But he was charmed by Roger. Roger was a young lawyer whose career had hardly started. Willie sat through a hilarious script of Roger's about working on the government's legal-aid scheme, representing people who were too poor to pay lawyers' fees. The poor people Roger had to deal with turned out to be querulous and crooked, and great lovers of the law. The script began and ended with the same fat old working woman coming to Roger's office and saying, 'Are you the poor lawyer?' The first time Roger had been solicitous. The second time he had sighed and said, 'Yes, that's me.'

Willie made his admiration plain during the recording and afterwards, and Roger took him to the BBC Club. When they were seated Roger said, 'I'm not actually a member. But it's convenient.'

Roger asked Willie about himself and Willie told him about the college of education.

Roger said, 'So you're going to be a teacher?'

Willie said, 'Not really.' And that was true. He had never intended to be a teacher. A phrase came to him: 'I'm marking time.'

Roger said, 'I'm like that, too.'

They became friends. Roger was tall and wore double-breasted dark suits. His manner, his style, his speech (easily veering into a curious formality, with complete, balanced sentences, creating for Willie an effect of wit) – all of this came to Roger from his family, his school, his university, his friends, his profession. But Willie saw it all as personal to Roger.

He saw one day that Roger wore trouser-braces. He was surprised. Roger said, when Willie asked him, 'No waist, no hips. Not like you, Willie. I just drop straight down.'

They met about once a week. Sometimes they had lunch at the Law Courts; Roger liked the puddings there. Sometimes they went to the theatre: Roger did a weekly 'London Letter' for a provincial paper and could get tickets for plays he wanted to write about. Sometimes they went to see the renovation work that was being done on a very small house, flat-fronted and low, that Roger had bought in a shabby street near Marble Arch. Roger, explaining the house, said, 'I had a little capital. Something under four thousand pounds. I thought the best thing was to put it in London property.' Roger was stressing the modesty of his means, explaining the very small house, but Willie was dazzled, not only by the four thousand pounds, but by Roger's confidence and knowledge, and by the words he had used, 'capital', 'property'. And just as, when he had walked down Kingsway to Bush House to record his talk about being an Indian Christian, there had come to Willie for the first time some idea of the wealth and power of pre-war England, so, gradually, out of his friendship with Roger, Willie felt he was seeing behind many blank doors, and there came to him the beginnings of an idea of England far removed from the boys in the college of education and the sensation-seekers of the immigrant-bohemian life of Notting Hill.

Percy Cato said one day, in an exaggerated Jamaican accent, 'Wha' happen, Willie-boy? Like somebody out there sweeten you up and you forgetting your old friend Percy.' Then in his normal voice he said, 'June's been asking about you.'

Willie thought about the room where she had taken him. She and Percy had no doubt often met there. He remembered the toilet, and the black man they had excited afterwards, fresh from the islands, the black man, still with the wide-brimmed Jamaican hat and his going-away tropical zoot-suit trousers. He saw it all from a distance now. In Roger's company it was more than ever like a secret.

Roger said, 'I still have no idea what you intend to do. Is there a family business? Are you one of the idle rich?'

Willie had learned to keep a straight face when embarrassing things were said and to walk round the embarrassment. He said, 'I want to write.' It wasn't true. The idea hadn't occurred to him until that moment, and it had occurred to him because Roger, embarrassing him, had made him think fast, and because he knew, from many things Roger had said, that he was a great reader and loved the contemporary English masters, Orwell, Waugh, Powell, Connolly.

Roger looked disappointed.

Willie said, 'Can I show you some things I've done?'

He typed out some of the stories he had done at the mission school. He took them to Roger's chambers one evening. They went to a pub and Roger read them across the table from Willie. Willie had never seen Roger look so serious. He thought, 'That's the lawyer.' And he was worried. He didn't care so much now about the stories, old things, after all. What he didn't want to lose was Roger's friendship.

At last Roger said, 'I know your great namesake and family friend says that a story should have a beginning, a middle and an end. But actually, if you think about it, life isn't like that. Life doesn't have a neat beginning and a tidy end. Life is always going on. You should begin in the middle and end in the middle, and it should all be there. This story about the brahmin and the treasure and the child sacrifice – it could have begun with the tribal chief coming to see the brahmin in his hermitage. He begins by threatening and ends by grovelling, but when he leaves we should know he is planning a terrible murder. Have you read Hemingway? You should read the early stories. There's one called "The Killers". It's only a few pages, almost all dialogue. Two men come at night to an empty cheap café. They take it over and wait for the old crook they've been hired to kill. That's all. Hollywood made a big film out of it, but the story is better. I know you wrote these stories at school. But you are pleased with them. What is interesting to me as a lawyer is that you don't want to write about real things. I've spent a fair amount of time listening to devious characters, and I feel about these stories that the writer has secrets. He is hiding.'

Willie was mortified. He burned with shame. He felt the tears coming. He reached across the table and took the stories back, and in the same movement he stood up.

Roger said, 'It's better to clear the air about certain things.'

Willie left the pub, thinking, 'I will never see Roger again. I shouldn't have shown him those old stories. He is right. That is the worst part.'

Grieving for the friendship, he began to think of June and the room in Notting Hill. He resisted the idea, but a few days later he went looking for her. He took the Underground to Bond Street. It was the lunch hour. As he was crossing the road to Debenhams he saw June and another girl coming in the opposite direction. She didn't see him. She was chattering away, head bent. Not like the steamy, silent, perfumed girl he remembered. Even her colour was different. Seeing her like this, with the other girl, almost in a domestic situation, her sexual tension gone, even her face slacker, Willie had no wish to greet her. They almost touched when they passed. She didn't see him. He could hear her gabbling words. He thought, 'This is how she is in Cricklewood. This is how she will be with everybody after a while.'

He felt relieved. But at the same time he felt cast out. It was like the time at home – long ago, as it now seemed – when he had begun to hate the mission school and had given up his old dream of becoming a missionary, someone of authority, and travelling the world.

Some days later he went to a bookshop. For two shillings and sixpence he bought a Penguin of early stories by Hemingway. He read the first four pages of 'The Killers' standing in the shop. He liked the vagueness of the setting and the general mysteriousness, and he thought the dialogue sang. It didn't sing so much in the later pages, when it became less mysterious; but Willie began to think that he should rewrite 'A Life of Sacrifice' in the way Roger had suggested.

The story, as he thought of it, became almost all dialogue. Everything was to be contained in the dialogue. The setting and the people weren't to be explained. That undid a lot of the difficulty. He had only to begin; the story rewrote itself; and though in one way it was now very far from Willie, it was also more full of his feelings. He changed the title to 'Sacrifice'.

Roger had mentioned the movie of 'The Killers'. Willie hadn't seen it. He wondered what they had done with the story. He tried idly to work it out. And, with his mind working in this way, it occurred to him over the next few days that there were scenes or even moments in Hollywood movies he might redo in the manner of 'Sacrifice', and with the vague 'Sacrifice' setting. He thought especially of the Cagney gangster movies and *High Sierra* with Humphrey Bogart. One of his first original compositions at the mission school had been something like that. He had written of a man (of no stated country or community) waiting for no stated reason in an undefined place for someone, smoking while he waited (there was a lot about cigarettes and matches), listening for motorcars and doors and footsteps. In the end (the composition was only a page long) the person had arrived, and the man waiting had become full of anger. He had ended it like that because he didn't have a story. He didn't know what had gone before or what was to come. But now, with the moments from the Cagney and Bogart movies, there wasn't this difficulty.

The stories came quickly to him. He wrote six in a week. *High Sierra* gave him three stories and he saw three or four more in it. He changed the movie character from story to story, so that the original Cagney or Bogart character became two or three different people. The stories were all in the same vague setting, the setting of *Sacrifice*. And as he wrote, the vague setting began to define itself, began to have markers: a palace with domes and turrets, a secretariat with lines of blank windows on three floors, a mysterious army cantonment with white-edged roads where nothing seemed to happen, a university with a yard and shops, two ancient temples where dressed-up crowds came on certain days, a market, housing colonies with graded dwellings, a hermitage with an unreliable holy man, an image-maker, and, outside the town, the high-smelling tanneries with their segregated population. To Willie's surprise, it was easier, with these borrowed stories far outside his own experience, and with these characters far outside himself, to be truer to his feelings than it had been with his cautious, half-hidden parables at school. He began to understand — and this was something they had had to write essays about at the college — how Shakespeare had done it, with his borrowed settings and borrowed stories, never with direct tales from his own life or the life around him.

The six stories came to no more than forty pages. And now that the first impulse had gone he wanted encouragement, and he thought of Roger. He wrote a letter, and Roger replied right away, asking Willie to lunch at Chez Victor in lower Wardour Street. Willie was early, and so was Roger. Roger

said, 'You saw the sign on the window? *Le patron mange içi.*
"The owner eats here." Literary people come here.' Roger
dropped his voice. 'The man across the way is V.S. Pritchett.'
Willie didn't know the name. The sturdy middle-aged man
was benign, with a well-modelled, humorous face and a
humorous, absent-minded air. Roger said, 'He writes the main
reviews for the *New Statesman*.' Willie had seen the magazine
in the college library, and he knew that there were college
students who competed for it every Friday morning. But
Willie had not yet developed the need to read magazines like
that. The *New Statesman* was to him a mystery, full of English
issues and references he didn't understand.

Roger said, 'My girlfriend is coming. Her name is Perdita.
She may even be my fiancée.'

The strange phrasing told Willie there was some trouble.
She was tall and slender, not beautiful, unremarkable, with a
slight awkwardness of posture. She was made up in a different
way from June, and something she had used had given a
shine to her pale skin. She took off her striped white gloves
and slapped them down together on the small Chez Victor
table with a sequence of gestures in which Willie saw such
style that he began to reconsider her face. And Willie soon
got to understand – such language of the eyes from Perdita,
such looking down and away by Roger – that, with all their
courtesies to each other and to him, the two people at his
table were not on good terms, and that he had been asked to
the lunch to act as a buffer.

The talk was mainly of the food. Some of it was about
Willie. Roger's courtesy never failed, but in Perdita's company
he looked extinguished, his eyes dull, his colour changed,

his openness gone, the beginnings of a vertical worry-line showing above the bridge of his nose.

He and Willie left Chez Victor together. Roger said, 'I am tired of her. And I will be tired of the one after her and the one after that. There's so *little* in a woman. And there's this myth about their beauty. It's their burden.'

Willie said, 'What does she want?'

'She wants me to go through with the business. Marry her, marry her, marry her. Whenever I look at her I feel I can hear the words.'

Willie said, 'I've been doing some writing. I've taken your advice. Would you like to read it?'

'Can we risk it?'

'I would like you to read it.'

He had the stories in the breast pocket of his jacket. He gave them to Roger. Three days later there was a friendly letter from Roger, and when they met Roger said, 'They are quite original. They are not like Hemingway at all. They are more like Kleist. One story on its own might not have an impact, but taken together they do. The whole sinister thing builds up. I like the background. It's India and not India. You should carry on. If you can do another hundred pages we might have to think of peddling it around.'

The stories didn't come so easily now, but they came, one a week, two a week. And whenever Willie felt he was running out of material, running out of cinematic moments, he went to see old movies or foreign movies. He went to the Everyman in Hampstead and the Academy in Oxford Street. He saw *The Childhood of Maxim Gorky* three times in one week at the Academy. He cried, fitting what he saw on the screen to his own childhood, and he wrote some stories.

* * *

ROGER SAID ONE DAY, 'My editor is coming to London soon. You know I do him a weekly letter about books and plays. I also drop the odd word about cultural personalities. He pays me ten pounds a week. I suppose he's coming to check on me. He says he wants to meet my friends. I've promised him an intellectual London dinner party, and you must come, Willie. It will be the first party in the Marble Arch house. I'll present you as a literary star to be. In Proust there's a social figure called Swann. He likes sometimes for his own pleasure to bring together dissimilar people, to create a social nosegay, as he says. I am hoping to do something like that for the editor. There'll be a Negro I met in West Africa when I did my National Service. He is the son of a West Indian who went to live in West Africa as part of the Back to Africa movement. His name is Marcus, after the black crook who founded the movement. You'll like him. He's very charming, very urbane. He is dedicated to inter-racial sex and is quite insatiable. When we first met in West Africa his talk was almost all about sex. To keep my end up I said that African women were attractive. He said, "If you like the animal thing." He is now training to be a diplomat for when his country becomes independent, and to him London is paradise. He has two ambitions. The first is to have a grandchild who will be pure white in appearance. He is half-way there. He has five mulatto children, by five white women, and he feels that all he has to do now is to keep an eye on the children and make sure they don't let him down. He wants when he is old to walk down the King's Road with this white grand-child. People will stare and the child will say, loudly, 'What are they staring at, Grandfather?' His second ambition is to be the first black man to have an account at Coutts. That's the Queen's bank.'

Willie said, 'Don't they have black people?'

'I don't know. I don't think he really knows either.'

'Why doesn't he just go to the bank and find out? Ask for a form.'

'He feels they might put him off in a discreet way. They might say they've run out of forms. He doesn't want that to happen. He will go to Coutts and ask to open an account only when he is sure that they'll take him. He wants to do it very casually, and he must be the first black man to do it. It's all very involved and I can't say I understand it. But you'll talk to him about it. He's quite open. It's part of his charm. There will also be a young poet and his wife. You should have no trouble with them. They will look disapproving and say absolutely nothing, and the poet will be waiting to snub anyone who talks to him. So you don't have to say anything to him. He is actually quite well known. My editor will be very pleased to meet him. In a foolish moment I wrote a friendly paragraph about one of the poet's books in a London Letter, and word somehow got back to him. That's how I've been landed with him.'

Willie said, 'I know about silent people. My father was always on a vow of silence. I'll look the poet up.'

'It won't give you any pleasure. The poetry is complicated

and showing off and perfectly arid, and you can think for some time that it's your fault it's like that. That's how I was taken in. Look him up if you want, but you mustn't feel you have to do it before the dinner. I'm asking the poet and his wife only for the nosegay effect. A little bit of dead fern, to set the whole thing off. The people you should study are two men I've known since Oxford. They are both of modest middle-class backgrounds and they pursue rich women. They do other things, but this is actually their career. Very rich women. It began in a small way at Oxford, and since then they have moved up and up, higher and higher, to richer and richer women. Their standards of wealth in a woman are now very high indeed. They are bitter enemies, of course. Each thinks the other is a fraud. It's been an education to see them operate. They both at about the same time in Oxford made the discovery that in the pursuit of rich women the first conquest is all-important. It piques the interest of other rich women, who might otherwise pay no attention to a middle-class adventurer, and it brings these women into the hunter's orbit. Soon the competition is among the rich women, each claiming to be richer than the others.

'Richard is ill-favoured and drunken and loud, and getting fat, not the kind of man you would think women would be attracted to. He wears grubby tweed jackets and dirty Viyella shirts. But he knows his market, and some of that coarseness is an act and is part of his bait. He presents himself as a kind of Bertolt Brecht, the promiscuous and smelly German communist playwright. But Richard is only a bedroom Marxist. Marxism takes him to the bedroom, and Marxism stops in the bedroom. All the women he seduces know that.

They feel safe with him. It was like that in Oxford and it's still like that. The difference is that at Oxford it thrilled his common soul just to sleep with rich women, and now he takes large sums of money off them. Of course he's made his mistakes. I imagine there has been more than one bedroom confrontation. I imagine a half-dressed lady saying tearfully, "I thought you were a Marxist." I imagine Richard pulling on his trousers fast and saying, "I thought you were rich." Richard is in publishing, quite rich now, and rising fast. As a publisher his Marxism makes him more attractive than ever. The more he takes off the ladies the more other ladies rush to give him.

'Peter's style is entirely different. His background is more modest, country estate agent, and at Oxford he began to develop his English-gentleman style. Oxford is full of young foreign women studying English at various language schools. Some of them are rich. Peter by some instinct ignored the university women and chose to operate among these people. They would have thought him the genuine article, and he, quicker than they, learning soon to sort the wheat from the chaff, scored some notable successes. He was invited to two or three rich European houses. He began to meet rich people on the Continent. He cultivated his appearance. He began to wear his hair in a kind of semi-military style, rising flat above the ears, and he learned to work his lantern jaws. One day in the junior common room, when we were having bad coffee after lunch, he said to me, "What would you say is the sexiest thing a man can wear?" I was taken aback. This wasn't typical common room conversation. But it showed how far Peter had got from estate-agenting, and where he was going. He said at last, "A very clean and well-ironed white shirt." A French girl he'd slept with the night before had told him that. And he's worn nothing but white shirts ever since. They are very expensive now, hand-made, very fine two-ply or three-ply cotton, the collar fitting close to his neck and riding well above the jacket at the back. He likes them starched in a certain way, so that the collar looks waxed. He is an academic, a historian. He's written a little book about food in history – an important subject, but a scrappy little anthology of a book – and he talks about new books and big advances from publishers, but that's only for show. His intellectual energy has actually become very low. The women consume him. To satisfy them he has developed what I can only describe as a special sexual taste. Women talk – never forget that, Willie – and word of this taste of Peter's has spread. It is now part of his success. His academic interests have always reflected the women he's been involved with. He's become a Latin-American expert, and now he's got a great prize. A Colombian woman. Colombia is a poor country, but she's connected to one of those absurd Latin-American fortunes that have been created out of four centuries of Indian blood and bones. She's coming with Peter, and Richard will be tormented by the most exquisite jealousy. He won't take it quietly. He will do something, create some fierce Marxist scene. I'll arrange it so that you talk to the lady. That's our nosegay. Our little dinner party for ten.'

Willie went away counting. He could only count nine. He wondered who the tenth person was.

On another day Roger said, 'My editor wants to stay with me. I've told him the house is very small, but he says he grew up in poverty and knows about back-to-back houses.

The house really has only a bedroom and a half. The editor is a very big man, and I suppose I will have to take the half bedroom. Or go to a hotel. That'll be unusual. I'll be like a guest at my own dinner party.'

On the day Willie knocked and waited for some time at the door of the little house. At last Perdita let him in. Willie didn't recognise her right away. The editor was already there. He was very fat, with glasses, bursting out of his shirt, and Willie felt it was his shyness, an unwillingness to be seen, that had made him not want to stay at a hotel. He seemed to take up a lot of room in the house, which in spite of all the little tricks of the architect was really very small. Roger, oppressed-looking, came up from the basement and did the introductions.

The editor remained sitting down. He said he saw Mahatma Gandhi in 1931 when the mahatma came to England for the Round Table Conference. He said nothing else about the mahatma (whom Willie and his mother and his mother's uncle despised), nothing about the mahatma's clothes or appearance; he spoke only of seeing him. When Marcus, the West Indian West African, came, the editor told in a similar way about seeing Paul Robeson.

Marcus looked confident and humorous and full of zest, and as soon as he began to talk Willie was captivated. Willie said, 'I've been hearing about your plans for a white grand-child.' Marcus said, 'It's not so extraordinary. It'll only be repeating something that happened on a large scale here a hundred and fifty years ago. In the eighteenth century there were about half a million black people in England. They've all vanished. They disappeared in the local population. They were bred out. The Negro gene is a recessive one. If this were more widely known there would be a good deal less racial feeling than there is. And a lot of that feeling is only skin deep, so to speak. I'll tell you this story. When I was in Africa I got to know a Frenchwoman from Alsace. She said after a time that she wanted me to meet her family. We went to Europe together and went to her home town. She introduced me to her school friends. They were conservative people and she was worried about what they would think. In the fortnight I was there I screwed them all. I even screwed two or three of the mothers. But my friend was still worried.'

The poet, when he came, received his homage from the editor, and then he and his wife sat sullenly together in one corner of the little room.

The Colombian woman was older than Willie expected. She might have been in her late forties. Her name was Serafina. She was slender, delicate, worried-looking. Her hair was black enough to suggest a dye, and her skin was very white and powdered up to the hair. When eventually she came and sat next to Willie she said, 'Do you like ladies?' When Willie hesitated she said, 'Not all men like ladies. I know. I was a virgin until I was twenty-six. My husband was a pederast. Colombia is full of little mestizo boys you can buy for a dollar.' Willie said, 'What happened when you were twenty-six?' She said, 'I am telling you my life story, but I am not in the confessional. Obviously something happened.' When Perdita and Roger began to pass the food around she said, 'I love men. I think they have a cosmic strength.' Willie said, 'You mean energy?' She said with irritation, 'I mean cosmic strength.' Willie looked at Peter. He had prepared for the evening. He was wearing his expensive-looking white shirt with the starched, waxy collar high at the back; his semi-military blond-and-grey hair was flat at the sides, with just a touch of pomade to keep it in order; but his eyes were dim and fatigued and far away.

Roger, passing with food, said, 'Why did you marry a pederast, Serafina?' She said, 'We are rich and white.' Roger said, 'That's hardly a reason.' She ignored that. She said, 'We have been rich and white for generations. We speak classical Spanish. My father was this white and handsome man. You should have seen him. It is hard for us to get married in Colombia.' Willie said, 'Aren't there other white people in Colombia?' Serafina said, 'It is a common word for you here. It isn't for us. We are rich and white in Colombia and we speak this pure old Spanish, purer than the Spanish they speak in Spain. It is hard for us to get husbands. Many of our girls have married Europeans. My younger sister is married to an Argentine. When you have to look so hard and so far for a husband you can make mistakes.'

Richard the publisher called out from across the room, 'I would say it's a mistake. Leaving Colombia and going to live on stolen Indian land.'

Serafina said, 'My sister has stolen no land.'

Richard said, 'It was stolen for her eighty years ago. By General Roca and his gang. The railway and the Remington rifle against Indian slings and stones. That's how the pampas were won, and all those bogus smart estancias. So your sister moved from old plunder to new theft. Thank God for Eva Perón, I say. Pulling down the whole rotten edifice.'

Serafina said to Willie, 'This man is trying to make himself interesting to me. It's a common type in Colombia.'

Marcus said, 'I don't think many people know that there were large Negro populations in Buenos Aires and Uruguay in 1800. They disappeared in the local population. They were bred out. The Negro is recessive. Not many people know that.'

Richard and Marcus carried on the cross-room talk, Richard always moving around what Marcus said and aiming to be provocative. Serafina said to Willie, 'He is the kind of man who will try to seduce me as soon as he is alone with me. It is boring. He thinks I am Latin American and easy.' She went silent. Through all of this Peter remained perfectly calm. Willie, no longer having to listen, and idly looking around the room, let his eyes rest on Perdita and her long upper body. He did not think her beautiful, but he remembered the elegant way she slapped the striped gloves down on the Chez Victor table, and at the same time he thought of June undressing in the room in Notting Hill. Perdita caught his gaze and held it. Willie was inexpressibly stirred.

Roger and Perdita began clearing away the plates. Marcus, in his brisk, zestful way, got up and began to help. Coffee and brandy came.

Serafina said absently to Willie, 'Have you felt jealousy?' Her thoughts had been running along ways he didn't know. Willie said, 'Not yet. I have only felt desire.' She said, 'Listen to this. When I took Peter to Colombia the women all ran to him. This English gentleman and scholar with the strong jaw-line. After one month he forgot everything I had done for him and he ran away with somebody else. But he didn't

know the country, and he made a big mistake. The woman
had fooled him. She was a mestiza and she wasn't rich at all.
He found out in a week. He came back to me and begged
to be forgiven. He knelt on the floor and put his head in
my lap and cried like a child. I stroked his hair and said,
"You thought she was rich? You thought she was white?"
He said, "Yes, yes." I forgave him. But perhaps he should be
punished. What do you think?'

The editor cleared his throat once, twice. It was his call
for silence. Serafina, turning away from Willie, and looking
away from Richard, sat up straight and fixed her gaze on the
editor. He sat big and heavy in his corner, overflowing
the waistband of his trousers, his shirt pulling at every button.

He said, 'I don't think any of you here can understand
what an occasion this evening has been for a provincial editor.
You have each one of you given me a glimpse of a world far
removed from my own. I come from a smoky old town in
the dark satanic north. Not many people want to know about
us nowadays. But we have played our part in history. Our
factories made goods that went all over the world, and wher-
ever our goods went they helped to usher in the modern
age. We quite rightly thought of ourselves as the centre of
the world. But now the world has tilted, and it is only when
I meet people like yourselves that I get some idea where the
world is going. So this occasion is full of ironies. You have
all led glittering lives. I have heard of some of you by
report, and everything I have seen and heard here tonight
has confirmed what I have heard. I wish from the bottom of
my heart to thank you all for the great courtesy you have
shown a man whose life has been the opposite of glittering.

But we who live in dark corners have our souls. We have had our ambitions, we have had our dreams, and life can play cruel tricks on us. "Perhaps in this neglected spot is laid some heart once pregnant with celestial fire." I cannot hope to match the poet Gray, but I have written in my own way of a heart like that. And I would like now, with your permission, and before we separate, perhaps for ever, to make you an offering of what I have written.'

From the inner breast pocket of his jacket the editor took out some folded sheets of newsprint. Deliberately, in the silence he had created, looking at no one, he shook out the sheets.

He said, 'These are galleys, newspaper proofs. The copy itself has been long prepared. A word or two may be changed here and there, an awkward phrase or two put right, but by and large it is ready for the press. It will be printed in my paper in the week of my death. You will guess that it is my obituary. Some of you may gasp. Some of you may sigh. But death comes to all, and it is better to be prepared. These words were composed in no spirit of vainglory. You know me well enough to know that. And it is, rather, in a spirit of sorrow, and regret for all the might-have-beens, that I invite you now to contemplate the course of an obscure provincial life.'

He began to read. '*Henry Arthur Percival Somers, who became editor of this paper in the dark days of November 1940, and whose death is reported more fully on another page, was born the son of a ship's fitter on 17 July 1895 . . .*'

Stage by stage, galley by galley, one narrow column of print to a galley, the story unfolded: the little house, the poor street, the father's periods of unemployment, family bereavements, the boy leaving school at fourteen, doing little clerking jobs in various offices, the war, his rejection by the army on medical grounds; and then at last, in the last year of the war, his job on the newspaper, on the production side, as a 'copy-holder', really a woman's job, reading copy aloud to the typesetter. As he read his emotion grew.

The poet and his wife looked on aloof and unsurprised and disdaining. Peter was vacant. Serafina held herself upright and showed her profile to Richard. Marcus, mentally restless, thinking of this and that, more than once began to talk about something quite unrelated, and then stopped at the sound of his own voice. But Willie was fascinated by the editor's story. To him it was all new. There were not many concrete details to hold on to, but he was trying as he listened to see the editor's town and to enter the editor's life. He found himself, to his surprise, thinking of his own father; and then he began to think about himself. Sitting beside Serafina, who had turned away from him, and was stiff, resisting conversation, Willie leaned forward to concentrate on the editor.

He, the editor, was aware of Willie's interest, and he weakened. He began to choke on his words. Once or twice he sobbed. And then he was on the last galley. Tears were running down his face. He seemed about to break down. ' . . . *His deepest life was in the mind. But journalism is by its nature ephemeral, and he left no memorial. Love, the divine illusion, never touched him. But he had a lifelong romance with the English language.*' He took off his misted glasses, held the galleys in his left hand, and fixed his wet eyes on a spot on the floor three or four feet in front of him. There was a great silence.

Marcus said, 'That was a very nice piece of writing.'

The editor remained as he had been, looking down at the floor, letting the tears flow, and silence came back to the room. The party was over. When people spoke, saying goodbye, it was in whispers, as in a sickroom. The poet and his wife left; it was as though they hadn't been. Serafina stood up, let her gaze sweep unseeing past Richard, and took Peter away. Marcus whispered, 'Let me help you clear away, Perdita.' Willie was surprised by a pang of jealousy. But neither he nor Marcus was allowed to stay.

Roger, saying goodbye to them at the door of the little house, lost his worried look. He said mischievously, not raising his voice, 'He told me he wanted to meet my London friends. I had no idea he wanted an audience.'

* * *

THE NEXT DAY Willie wrote a story about the editor. He set it in the quarter-real Indian town he used in his writing, and he fitted the editor to the holy man he had already written about in some of the stories. Up to this point the holy man had been seen from the outside: idle and sinister, living off the unhappy, waiting like a spider in his hermitage. Now, unexpectedly, the holy man showed his own unhappiness: imprisoned in his way of life, longing to get away from his hermitage, and telling his story to a seeker from far away, someone passing through, unlikely to return. In mood the story was like the story the editor had told. In substance it was like the story Willie had heard over many years from his father.

The story, growing under his hand, took Willie by surprise. It gave him a new way of looking at his family and his life, and over the next few days he found the matter of many stories of a new sort. The stories seemed to be just waiting for him; he was surprised he hadn't seen them before; and he wrote fast for three or four weeks. The writing then began to lead him to difficult things, things he couldn't face, and he stopped.

It was the end of his writing. Nothing more came. The movie inspiration had dried up some time before. While it had held it had seemed so easy that sometimes he had worried that other people might be doing the same thing: getting story ideas, or dramatic moments, from *High Sierra* and *White Heat* and *The Childhood of Maxim Gorky*. Now, when nothing was happening, he wondered how he had done what he had done. He had written twenty-six stories in all. They came to about a hundred and eighty pages, and he was disappointed that so many ideas and so much writing and so much excitement had produced so few pages.

But Roger thought it a fair size for a book, and he thought the collection complete. He said, 'The later stories are more inward, but I like that. I like the way the book grows and spreads. It's more mysterious and more full of feeling than you know, Willie. It's very good. But please don't think it means fame.'

Roger began to send the book out to people he knew in publishing. Every two or three weeks it came back.

Roger said, 'It's as I feared. Short stories are always

difficult, and India isn't really a subject. The only people who are going to read about India are people who have lived or worked there, and they are not going to be interested in the India you write about. The men want John Masters – *Bhowani Junction* and *Bugles and a Tiger* – and the women want *Black Narcissus* by Rumer Godden. I didn't want to send it to Richard, but it looks as though he's the only one left.'

Willie said, 'Why don't you want to send it to Richard?'

'He's a scoundrel. He can't help it. He will find some way of doing you down. It's his attitude to the world. Always has been. He likes doing the crooked thing almost for sport. And if he does the book he will present it in his doctrinaire way, using the book to make some Marxist point. It will help his Marxist reputation, but it won't help the book. But needs must when the devil drives.'

So the book went to Richard. And he took it. A letter on the firm's paper came to Willie at the college, asking him to make an appointment to come to the office.

It was in one of the black Bloomsbury squares. It was the kind of London building – flat-fronted, black-bricked – that seemed ordinary to Willie. Yet as he went up the front steps the building, which had seemed small, appeared to get bigger. At the front door he saw that the building was really large and fine, and when he was inside he saw that behind the black front were high, well-lighted rooms that went far back.

In the reception room the girl at the switchboard was in a panic. A voice was booming at her from the equipment. Willie recognised the voice as Richard's. It was bullying without any effort, and it made the thin-armed girl frantic. She might have been at home, not in a public place, and the voice might have reminded her of a threatening or violent father. Willie thought of his sister Sarojini. It was a little while before the girl noticed Willie, and it took her some time to compose herself to talk to him.

Richard's office was the front room on the first floor. It was a big, high room, with a wall of books.

Richard walked Willie to the high windows and said, 'These houses used to be the houses of rich London merchants a hundred and fifty years ago. One of the houses in this square might very well have been the Osborne house in *Vanity Fair*. The room where we are would have been the drawing room. Even now you can look out and imagine the carriages and footmen and all the rest. What is hard nowadays to imagine, and what most people forget, is that Thackeray's great London merchant, sitting in a room like this, wanted his son to marry a Negro heiress from St Kitts in the West Indies. I've been working in this building for many years, but it wasn't something I carried in my mind. It was your friend Marcus who reminded me. The man who wants to open an account at Coutts. It sounded like a joke when he told me about the heiress, but I checked up. The lady's fortune would have come from slaves and sugar. Those were the great days of the West Indian slave plantations. Imagine. At a time like that, a Negro heiress in London. And she was greatly in demand. She would have married well, of course, though Thackeray doesn't tell us. And, the Negro gene being as recessive as it is, in a couple of generations her descendants would have been perfectly English and upper class. It takes a resettled black man from West Africa to give us this corrective reading of one of our Victorian classics.'

They left the window and went and sat on opposite sides of the big desk. Richard, sitting down, was wider and heavier and coarser than Willie remembered.

Richard said, 'One day you might give us a new reading of *Wuthering Heights*. Heathcliff was a half-Indian child who was found near the docks of Liverpool. But you know that.' He took up some typed sheets. 'This is the contract for your book.'

Willie took out his pen.

Richard said, 'Aren't you going to read it?'

Willie was confused. He wanted to look at the contract, but he didn't feel he could tell Richard that. To want to read through the contract in Richard's presence would be to question Richard's honour, and that would be such a discourtesy that Willie couldn't do it.

Richard said, 'It's pretty much our standard contract. Seven and a half per cent on home sales, three and a half per cent on overseas sales. We'll handle the other rights for you. We are assuming, of course, that you'll want that. If we sell it in America, you'll get sixty-five per cent. You'll get sixty per cent for translations, fifty if we sell to the films, forty for the paperback. You may feel at this stage that these rights are of no consequence. But they shouldn't be let go. We'll do the hard work for you. It's what we are equipped to do. You'll sit back and rake in whatever comes.'

There were two copies of the contract for Willie to sign. When he was signing the second copy Richard took out an envelope from the drawer of the desk and put it in front of him.

Richard said, 'It's the advance. Fifty pounds, in new five-pound notes. Have you ever earned more at one time?'

Willie hadn't. His largest radio fee had been thirteen guineas, for a fifteen-minute script on *Oliver Twist* for the BBC Schools Transcription Service.

When he went down the girl at the switchboard was calmer. But the wretchedness of her life – caught between tormenting office and tormenting house – showed on her face. Willie thought, in a more helpless, despairing way than before, of his sister Sarojini at home.

Roger wanted to see the contract. Willie was nervous about that. He would have found it hard to explain to Roger why he had signed. Roger became serious and lawyer-like as he read, and at the end he said, after a slight hesitation, 'I suppose the main thing is to get it published. What did he say about the book? He is usually very intelligent about these things.'

Willie said, 'He didn't say anything about the book. He talked about Marcus and *Vanity Fair*.'

Four or five weeks later there was a party at Richard's house in Chelsea. Willie went early. He saw no one that he knew, and became involved with a short, fat man, quite young – with glasses and uncombed hair, a too-small jacket and a dirty pullover – who appeared to be living up to some antique bohemian idea of the writer. He was a psychologist and had written a book called *The Animal in You – and Me*. Some copies of it were about; no one was paying much attention to it. Willie was so taken up with this man – each using the other to take cover from the indifferent room – that Willie didn't see Roger arrive. Almost as soon as he saw Roger he saw Serafina. She was with Richard. She was in a pink dress with a flower pattern, upright and elegant, but not as severe as at Roger's dinner. Willie left the psychologist and moved towards her. She was easy and warm with him, and quite attractive in her new mood. But all her thoughts were for Richard. They were talking – in an oblique way, and through interruptions – of some bold business project they were doing together: going first into the paper-making business in Jujuy in the north of Argentina and later printing paperback books more cheaply than in Europe and the United States. It was possible now to make good-quality paper out of bagasse. Bagasse was the stringy pith that remained after sugar-cane was crushed to make sugar. Serafina had many square miles of sugar-cane land in Jujuy. Bagasse in Jujuy cost nothing; it was waste; and sugar-cane grew in less than a year.

Well-dressed men and carefully dressed women, using words and smiles to say very little, moved around this – slightly showing-off – conversation about bagasse.

Willie thought, 'In that big office Richard was real. And the girl was real. Here in this small house, at this party, Richard is acting. Everybody is acting.'

Afterwards Roger and Willie talked about the party and about Serafina.

Roger said, 'Richard will take a few hundred thousand off her. It's his talent, to come up with these attractive projects. The bizarre thing is that if someone actually applied himself, many of Richard's projects could make money. He himself is not interested in the working out of anything. He doesn't have the patience. He likes the excitement of the idea, the snare, the quick money. And then he moves on. Serafina is already very excited. So in a way it doesn't matter if she doesn't get her money back. She will have had her excitement. And she hasn't earned her money. It was earned for her a long time ago. It is what Richard will tell her when she complains. If she complains.'

Willie said, using a word he had got from the college, 'There were some very classy people there.'

Roger said, 'They've all written books. It's the last infirmity of the powerful and the high-born. They don't actually want to write, but they want to be writers. They want their name on the back of a book. Richard, in addition to everything else, is a very high-class vanity publisher. People pay a vanity publisher to bring out their books. Richard doesn't do anything so crude. He is so very discreet and so very selective with his vanity publishing that nobody actually knows. And he has any number of rich and well-placed people who are grateful to him. In some ways he is as powerful as a cabinet minister. They come and go, but Richard goes on. He advances through society in all directions.'

For many weeks Willie had been in and out of Roger's house at Marble Arch, taking advice during the preparation of the manuscript and then talking over the rejection letters. Perdita had often been there. Her elegance had grown on Willie, and for some time, through all the talk about the book and publishers, Willie had been embarrassed with Roger. He wanted to make a full declaration to Roger, but he didn't have the courage. Now that the book had been placed, and he had got his fifty pounds, he thought it dishonourable to delay any longer. He thought he would go to Roger's chambers, for the formality, and say, 'Roger, I have something to say to you. Perdita and I are in love.'

But he never went to Roger's chambers. Because that weekend the race riots began in Notting Hill. The silent streets – with exposed rubbish bins daubed with house and flat numbers, and with windows heavily curtained and screened and blank – became full of excited people. The houses that had seemed tenanted only by the very old and passive now let out any number of young men in mock-Edwardian clothes who roamed the streets looking for blacks. A West Indian called Kelso, with no idea of what was happening, coming to visit friends, walked into a teenage crowd outside Latimer Road Underground station and was killed.

The newspapers and the radio were full of the riots. On the first day Willie went, as he often did, to the little café near the college for mid-morning coffee. It seemed to him that everyone was reading the newspapers. They were black with photographs and headlines. He heard a small old working man, years of deprivation on his face, say casually, as he might have done at home, 'Those blacks are going to be a menace.' It was a casual remark, not at all reflecting what was in the papers, and Willie felt at once threatened and ashamed. He felt people were looking at him. He felt the newspapers were about him. After this he stayed in the college and didn't go out. This kind of hiding wasn't new to him. It was what they used to do at home, when there was serious religious or caste trouble.

On the third day of the riots a telegram came from the radio producer he knew. It asked him to telephone.

The producer said, 'Willie. This is something we just have to do. People all over the world are waiting to see whether we will do this story or not, and how we will do it. My idea is like this, Willie. You will go in your ordinary clothes to Ladbroke Grove or St Ann's Well Road or Latimer Road Underground. Latimer Road will be better. That's where the main trouble was. Your attitude will be that of a man from India who has come to have a look at Notting Hill. You want to see what Kelso found. So you go looking for the crowds. You're a little bit a man looking for trouble, a man looking to be beat up. Only up to a point, of course. That's all. See what transpires. The usual five-minute script.'

'What's the fee?'

'Five guineas.'

'That's what you always pay. This isn't a fashion show or an art exhibition.'

'We have a budget, Willie. You know that.'

Willie said, 'I have exams. I am revising. I don't have the time.'

A letter came from Roger. *Dear Willie, In the life of great cities there are always moments of madness. Other things do not alter. You must know that Perdita and I are always here for you.* Willie thought, 'He's a good man. Perhaps the only one I know. Some good instinct made me seek him out after he had done that broadcast about being a legal-aid lawyer. I am glad I didn't go to his chambers and tell him about Perdita.'

Hiding away in the college, Willie now saw more of

Percy Cato than he had done for some months. They were still friends but their different interests had made them move apart. Willie knew more of London now, and didn't need to have Percy as a guide and support. Those bohemian parties with Percy and June and the others – and, as well, some of the lost, the unbalanced, the alcoholic, the truly bohemian – those parties in shabby Notting Hill flats no longer seemed metropolitan and dazzling.

Percy was as stylish in his dress as always. But his face had changed; he had lost some of his bounce.

He said, 'The old man's going to lose his manor after this. The papers won't let him go now. But he's trying to take me down with him. He can be very nasty. He's never forgiven me for turning my back on him. The press has been digging up things about the old man's properties and development schemes in Notting Hill, and somebody is spreading a story that I was his black right-hand man. Every day I open the papers in the common room and expect to see my name. The college wouldn't like it. Giving a scholarship to a black Notting Hill crook. They might ask me to leave. And I wouldn't know where to go, Willie.'

A letter came to Willie from India. Envelopes from home had a special quality. They were of local recycled paper, suggesting the junk from which they had been made, and they would have been put together in the bazaar, in the back rooms of the paper stalls, by poor boys sitting on the floor, some of them using big-bladed paper-cutters (not far from their toes), some using glue brushes. Willie could easily imagine himself back there, without hope. For that reason the first sight of these letters from home was depressing, and the depression could stay with him, its cause forgotten, after he had read the letter.

The handwriting on this letter was his father's. Willie thought, with the new tenderness he had begun to feel for his father, 'The poor man's heard about the riots and he's worried. He thinks they are like the riots at home.'

He read: *Dear Willie, I hope this finds you as it leaves me. I don't normally write because I don't normally have news, at least not of the sort I feel I should write to you about. I write now with news of your sister Sarojini. I do not know what your reaction will be. You know that people come to the ashram from all over. Well, a German came one day. He was an oldish man with a bad leg. Well, to cut a long story short, he asked to marry Sarojini, and that is precisely what he has done. You will know that I always felt that Sarojini's only hope lay in an international marriage, but I must say this took me by surprise. I am sure he has a wife somewhere, but perhaps it isn't good to ask too much. He is a photographer, and he talks of fighting in Berlin at the end of the war, firing a machine-gun at the Russian tanks while his friend had thrown away his gun and was flat on the ground, chattering with fright. These days he makes films about revolutions, and that's how he makes a living. It's unusual, but these days everybody finds his own way* – Willie thought, 'You can say that again' – *and of course you will say that I am the last person to talk. They are going to make a film about Cuba. It's the place where they make cigars. They are going to be with a man with a Goan kind of name, Govia or Govara, and then they will be going to other places. Your mother is quite glad to get the girl off her hands, but it will be no surprise to you that she is pretending she isn't. I don't know where this thing will end or how it will work out for poor Sarojini. Well, that's all the news for now.*

Willie thought, 'It's something I have learned since I came here. Everything goes on a bias. The world should stop, but it goes on.'

THREE

A Second Translation

IT OCCURRED TO WILLIE one day that he hadn't seen Percy Cato at the college for some time. When he asked around he heard that Percy had packed his bags and left the college without telling anyone. No one could say where Percy was, but a story was that he had left London and gone back to Panama. Willie was forlorn at the news. It was as though – especially after the riots in Notting Hill – all the early part of his life in London was now lost. Percy had said that he was worried about his name appearing in the papers. But though the papers wrote a lot for some weeks about property racketeers in Notting Hill, they didn't seem to know about Percy; and Willie felt that Percy had decided to leave London because in his usual wise way he had had an inkling of something more terrible to come. Willie felt left behind and exposed. The savour went out of his London life, and he began to wonder, as he had done at the very beginning, where he was going.

His sister Sarojini wrote from Germany. Willie didn't want to open the envelope. He remembered, with shame, how it would have excited him at home, at the ashram or the mission school, to see a German or any foreign postage stamp on a letter. The design of the stamp would have set him dreaming of the country, and he would have thought the sender of the letter blessed.

Dear Willie, I wonder if you know what worry you're giving us. You do not write and we have no idea what you are doing. Can you take a degree at this college where you are, and will that degree get you a job? You have the example of your father before you, and if you aren't careful you will become an idler like him. Things work like that in families.

Willie thought, 'I used to worry about this girl. I didn't think she had a chance, and I would have done anything to help her become a happy woman. Then this old German man comes along and ugly little Sarojini changes. She becomes the complete married woman, as though that woman was there all along. She has become just like my mother. I feel as if all my worry and love has been mocked. I am not sure I like this Sarojini.'

Wolf and I are about to go to Cuba and other places. Wolf has talked to me a lot about revolutionary ideas. He is like our mother's uncle, but of course he has had more opportunities and is better educated, and of course he has seen much more of the world than our poor uncle. I wish you could take after that side of the family, and then you will see how much there is to do in our world, and how you are selfishly wasting your life in London doing this little thing and that little thing and not knowing why you are doing anything. Wolf and I are in Germany for a few weeks. Wolf has film people and government people to see here.

*When things settle down I will come to London for a few days
to see you.*

Willie thought, 'Please don't come, Sarojini. Please don't
come.'

But in due course she came, and for three or four days
she turned his life upside down. She stayed in a small hotel
near the college – she had arranged that herself, before she
left Germany – and she came every day to Willie's college
room and prepared a rough little meal. She asked for his
help in nothing. She bought cheap new pots and pans and
knives and spoons, found out about greengrocers, came in
every day with fresh vegetables, and cooked things on the
little electric heater in Willie's room. She laid the heater on
its back and she set the pots on the metal guards above the
glowing electric coils. They ate off paper plates and she
washed up the pots in the sink at the end of the corridor.
Sarojini had never been a good cook, and the food she cooked
in the college room was awful. The smell stayed in the room.
Willie was worried about breaking the college rules, and he was
just as worried about people seeing the dark little cook –
clumsily dressed: with a cardigan over her sari and socks on
her feet – who was his sister. In her new assertive way, but
still not knowing too much about anything, in five minutes
she would have babbled away all Willie's careful little stories
about their family and background.

She said, 'When you get this famous degree or diploma,
what will you do with it? You will get a little teaching job
and hide away here for the rest of your life?'

Willie said, 'I don't think you know. But I've written a
book. It's coming out next year.'

'That's a lot of nonsense. Nobody here or anywhere else will want to read a book by you. I don't have to tell you that. Remember when you wanted to be a missionary?'

'What I mean is that I feel I should wait here until the book comes out.'

'And then there'll be something else to wait for, and then there'll be something after that. This is your father's life.'

For days after she left the smell of her cooking was in Willie's room. At night Willie smelt it on his pillow, his hair, his arms.

He thought, 'What she says is right, though I don't like her for saying it. I don't know where I am going. I am just letting the days go by. I don't like the place that's waiting for me at home. For the past two and a half years I have lived like a free man. I can't go back to the other thing. I don't like the idea of marrying someone like Sarojini, and that's what will happen if I go home. If I go home I will have to fight the battles my mother's uncle fought. I don't want to fight those battles. It will be a waste of my precious life. There are others who would enjoy those battles. And Sarojini is right in the other way too. If I get my teaching diploma and decide to stay here and teach it will be a kind of hiding away. And it wouldn't be nice teaching in a place like Notting Hill. That's the kind of place they would send me, and I would walk with the fear of running into a crowd and being knifed like Kelso. It would be worse than being at home. And if I stay here I would always be trying to make love to my friends' girlfriends. I have discovered that that is quite an easy thing to do. But I know it to be wrong, and it would get me into trouble one day. The trouble is I don't know how to go out and get a girl on my own. No one trained me in that. I don't know how to make a pass at a stranger, when to touch a girl or hold her hand or try to kiss her. When my father told me his life story and talked about his sexual incompetence I mocked him. I was a child then. Now I discover I am like my poor father. All men should train their sons in the art of seduction. But in our culture there is no seduction. Our marriages are arranged. There is no art of sex. Some of the boys here talk to me about the Kama Sutra. Nobody talked about that at home. It was an upper-caste text, but I don't believe my poor father, brahmin though he is, ever looked at a copy. That philosophical-practical way of dealing with sex belongs to our past, and that world was ravaged and destroyed by the Muslims. Now we live like incestuous little animals in a hole. We grope all our female relations and are always full of shame. Nobody talked about sex and seduction at home, but I discover now that it is the fundamental skill all men should be trained in. Marcus and Percy Cato, and Richard, seemed to be marvellous that way. When I asked Percy how he had learned he said he started small, fingering and then raping little girls. I was shocked by that. I am not so shocked now.'

He telephoned Perdita early one morning. 'Perdita, please come to the college this weekend.'

'This is foolish, Willie. And it's not fair to Roger.'

'It isn't fair. But I have a need of you. I was bad the last time. But I'll tell you. It's a cultural matter. I want to make love to you, want desperately to make love to you, but then at the actual moment old ideas take over and I become

ashamed and frightened, I don't know of what, and it all goes
bad. I'll be better this time. Let me try.'

'Oh, Willie. You've said that before.'

She didn't come.

He went looking for June. He hadn't seen her for some
months. He wondered what had happened to the house in
Notting Hill, and whether, after the riots, it would still be
possible for them to go there. But June wasn't at the perfume
counter in Debenhams. The other girls, with their too made-
up faces, were not friendly. One or two even shrank back
from him: it might have been the determined, hard-heeled
way he had walked up to them. At last he met a girl who
gave him news of June. June was married. She had married
her childhood sweetheart, someone she had known since she
was twelve. The girl telling Willie the story was still full of
the romance of the whole thing, and her eyes had a genuine
glitter below the false eyelashes and the mascara and the
painted eyebrow lines. 'They went everywhere together. They
were like brother and sister. He is in a funny business, though.
Undertaker. Family business. But if you grow up in it it's
different, June said. He and June sometimes did funerals
together. They had an old Rolls-Royce for the wedding. Her
family hired it for twenty-five pounds. A lot of money, but
it was worth it. June saw the pretty car in the morning. The
local man who rented it out was driving. Peaked cap and
everything. She said to her father, "You haven't hired it, have
you?" He said no, it was probably just going to a vintage-
car rally. And then of course it was there. Like brother and
sister they were. It isn't the kind of thing that happens often
these days.'

Half a Life

The more the girl talked, the more she gave Willie pictures of the safe life in Cricklewood, the life of family and friends, the pleasures and excitements, the more Willie felt cast out, lost. If Willie had learned to drink – and had learned the style connected with drink – he might have gone to a pub. He thought instead of finding a prostitute.

He went very late that evening to Piccadilly Circus. He walked around the side streets, hardly daring to look at the aggressive, dangerous-looking streetwalkers. He walked until he was tired. At about midnight he went into a bright café. It was full of prostitutes, hard, foolish-looking, not attractive, most of them drinking tea and smoking, some of them eating soft white cheese rolls. They talked in difficult accents. One girl said to another, 'I've got five left.' She was talking about french letters. She took them out of her bag and counted them. Willie went out and walked again. The streets were quieter. In a side street he saw a girl talking to a man in a friendly way. Out of interest he walked towards them. Suddenly an angry man shouted, 'What the hell do you think you are doing?' and crossed the road. He wasn't shouting at Willie but at the girl. She broke away from the man she was talking to. She had a kind of glitter dust on her hair, her forehead, her eyelids. She said to the bald shouting man, 'I know him. He was in the RAF when I was in the WAAF.'

Later, out of a wish not to be utterly defeated, Willie talked to a woman. He didn't consider her face. He just followed her. It was awful for him in the over-heated little room with smells of perfume and urine and perhaps worse. He didn't look at the woman. They didn't talk. He concentrated on himself, on undressing, on his powers. The woman

A Second Translation

only half undressed. She said to Willie in a rough accent,
'You can keep your socks on.' Strange words, heard often
before, but never with such a literal meaning. She said, 'Be
careful with my hair.' An erection came to Willie, an erection
without sensation, and, joylessly, it didn't go. Willie was
ashamed. He remembered some words from the old Pelican
book about sex, words that had once rebuked him. He
thought, 'Perhaps I have become a sexual athlete.' At that
moment the woman said to him, 'Fuck like an Englishman.'
A few seconds later she threw him off. He didn't want to
argue. He dressed and went back to the college. He was full
of shame.

Some days later, travelling on a bus past the Victoria coach
station, the terminus for buses to the provinces, he saw as
clear as day the prostitute to whom he had given half a week's
allowance. She was dumpy, plain, unremarkable without the
make-up of the night and the pretence of vice, someone
clearly who had come up from the provinces to do a few
nights in London, and was now going back home.

Willie thought, 'Humiliation like this awaits me here. I
must follow Percy. I must leave.'

He had no idea where he might go. Percy – with less of
a start in the world, with a father who had left Jamaica to
join the faceless black gangs working on the Panama Canal
– had the advantage on him there. Percy could go to Panama
or Jamaica or, if he wanted to, the United States. Willie could
only go back to India, and he didn't want that. All that he
had now was an idea – and it was like a belief in magic –
that one day something would happen, an illumination would
come to him, and he would be taken by a set of events to

the place he should go. What he had to do was to hold himself in readiness, to recognise the moment.

In the meantime there was the book to wait for, and the diploma to get. He hid away in the college and, thinking of his liberation rather than the college diploma as the true reward of his labour, he worked at the dull textbooks. And it seemed that, as he was seeking to forget the world, so just then he was forgotten by the world. No request from the BBC producer for a script, no note from Roger, nothing for some weeks to remind him that he had made an active and mixed London life for himself and was an author with a book soon to be published. Richard's catalogue came, to remind him. It was depressing. The book had a paragraph on a half-page somewhere in the middle. Willie was presented as 'a subversive new voice from the subcontinent', and there was something about the unusual Indian provincial setting of the stories, but there was no further clue to the nature of the writing. The catalogue entry, modest, even bleak, commercially self-denying, seemed less a tribute to the book than a tribute to Richard and the well-known politics of his firm. This was the side of Richard that Roger had been worried about. Willie felt that his book was tainted, lost to him, and already dead. A little while later the proofs came. He worked on them like a man going through the rites and formalities connected with a stillbirth. About four months after that the six copies of the published book arrived.

There was nothing from Richard or his office. There was nothing from Roger: Willie feared that Perdita had given him away. He felt himself sinking in this silence. He looked through the newspapers and the weeklies in the college library.

He looked at publications he had never read. He saw nothing about his book for two weeks, and then here and there, low among the notices of new fiction, he began to see small paragraphs.

... *Where, after the racy Anglo-Indian fare of John Masters, one might have expected an authentic hot curry, one gets only a nondescript savoury, of uncertain origin, and one is left at the end with the strange sensation of having eaten variously and at length but of having missed a meal* ...

... *These random, unresolved pieces of terror or disquiet or anxiety seem in the most unsettling way to come out of no settled view of the world. They speak volumes of the disorientation of the young, and they augur ill for the new state* ...

Willie thought, 'Let the book die. Let it fade away. Let me not be reminded of it. I will write no more. This book was not something I should have done, anyway. It was artificial and false. Let me be grateful that none of the reviewers spotted the way it was done.'

And then one day he had two letters. One was from Roger. *Dear Willie, Belated congratulations on the book, which of course I know very well. The reviews I have seen haven't been at all bad. It's not an easy book to write about. Each reviewer seems to have touched on a different aspect of the book. And that's pretty good. Richard should have done more, but that's his style. Books have their destiny, as the Latin poet says, and I feel that your book will live in ways you cannot at the moment imagine.* In his defeated mood, and with his worry about Perdita, Willie saw ambiguities in the letter. He thought it cool and distant, and he didn't feel he should acknowledge it.

The other letter was from a girl or young woman from

an African country. She had a Portuguese-sounding name and she was doing a course of some sort in London. She said that the review in the *Daily Mail* – a poor one, Willie remembered, but the reviewer had tried to describe the stories – had made her get the book. *At school we were told that it was important to read, but it is not easy for people of my background and I suppose yours to find books where we can see ourselves. We read this book and that book and we tell ourselves we like it, but all the books they tell us to read are written for other people and really we are always in somebody else's house and we have to walk carefully and sometimes we have to stop our ears at the things we hear people say. I feel I had to write to you because in your stories for the first time I find moments that are like moments in my own life, though the background and material are so different. It does my heart a lot of good to think that out there all these years there was someone thinking and feeling like me.*

She wanted to meet him. He at once wrote to her asking her to come to the college. And then he was worried. She might not be as nice as her letter. He knew almost nothing about her Portuguese African country, nothing about the races and groupings and tensions. She had mentioned her background but not said anything about it. It was possible that she belonged to a mixed community or stood in some other kind of half-and-half position. Something like that would explain her passion, the way she had read his book. Willie thought of his friend Percy Cato, now lost to him: jokey and foppish on the surface, but full of rages underneath. But if she came and questioned him too closely about his book he might find himself giving the game away, and the woman or girl with the Portuguese-sounding name might understand that the Indian stories in which she had seen aspects of her own African life had been borrowed from old Hollywood movies and the Maxim Gorky trilogy from Russia. Willie didn't want the woman to be let down. He wanted her to stay an admirer. This line of thinking led him the other way, to worrying about himself. He began to worry that the woman might not find him good enough for the book he had written, not attractive enough or with presence enough.

But as soon as he saw her all his anxieties fell away, and he was conquered. She behaved as though she had always known him, and had always liked him. She was young and small and thin, and quite pretty. She had a wonderfully easy manner. And what was most intoxicating for Willie was that for the first time in his life he felt himself in the presence of someone who accepted him completely. At home his life had been ruled by his mixed inheritance. It spoilt everything. Even the love he felt for his mother, which should have been pure, was full of the pain he felt for their circumstances. In England he had grown to live with the idea of his difference. At first this feeling of difference had been like a liberation from the cruelties and rules of home. But then he had begun in certain situations – with June, for instance, and then Perdita, and sometimes when there was trouble at the college – to use his difference as a weapon, making himself simpler and coarser than he was. It was the weapon he was ready to use with the girl from Africa. But there was no need. There was, so to speak, nothing to push against, no misgiving to overcome, no feeling of distance.

After half an hour the spell didn't break, and Willie began to luxuriate in this new feeling of being accepted as a man and being in his own eyes complete. It might have been the book that made her look on him in this unquestioning way. It might have been Ana's mixed African background. Willie didn't wish to probe, and what Ana gave him he returned in full measure. He was entranced by the girl and over the next few weeks learned to love everything about her: her voice, her accent, her hesitations over certain English words, her beautiful skin, the authority with which she handled money. He had seen that way with money on no other woman. Perdita always got lost when she looked for money; big-hipped June waited until the very end of a transaction before taking out and opening a small purse with her big hands. Ana always had money ready. And with that air of authority there was her nervous thinness. That thinness made him feel protective. It was easy to make love to her, and he was tender then in the way that was natural to him, with nothing of the aggression Percy Cato had recommended; and everything that had been hard before, with the others, was pure pleasure with her.

The first time they kissed – on the narrow sofa facing the electric heater in his college room – she said, 'You should look after your teeth. They are spoiling your looks.' He said, as a joke, 'I dreamt the other night that they had become very heavy and were about to drop out.' And it was true: he had been careless of his teeth since he had been in England, and he had altogether neglected them after the Notting Hill riots and Percy Cato's disappearance and the dismissing paragraph about his book in Richard's wretched catalogue. He had even begun to take a kind of pleasure in the staining, almost now the blackness, of his teeth. He tried to tell her

the story. She said, 'Go to the dentist.' He went to an Australian dentist in Fulham and told him, 'I have never been to
a dentist. I feel no pain. I have no problem to talk to you
about. I've come to you only because I have been dreaming
that I am about to lose my teeth.' The dentist said, 'We're
ready even for that. And it's all on the National Health. Let's
have a look.' And then he told Willie, 'That wasn't a dream
with a hidden meaning, I'm afraid. Your teeth really were
going to fall out. Tartar like concrete. And horribly stained
– you must drink a lot of tea. The lower teeth mortared
together, a solid wall of the stuff. I've never seen anything
like it. It's a wonder you were able to lift your jaw.' He went
at the tartar with relish, scraping and chipping and grinding,
and when he was finished Willie's mouth felt sore and his
teeth felt exposed and shaky and sensitive even to the air. He
said to Ana, 'I've been hearing funny things from the boys
at the college about Australian dentists in London. I hope
we've done the right thing.'

He encouraged Ana to talk about her country. He tried to
visualise the country on the eastern coast of Africa, with the
great emptiness at its back. Soon, from the stories she told,
he began to understand that she had a special way of looking
at people: they were African or not African. Willie thought,
'Does she just see me then as someone who's not an African?'
But he pushed that idea to one side.

She told a story about a school friend. 'She always wanted
to be a nun. She ended up in an order somewhere here, and
I went to see her some months ago. They live a kind of jail
life. And, like people in jail, they keep in touch in their own
way with the world outside. At mealtimes somebody reads

selected items from the newspaper to them, and they giggle like schoolgirls at the simplest jokes. I could have cried. That beautiful girl, that wasted life. I couldn't help myself, I asked her why she had done it. It was wrong of me, adding to her sorrows. She said, "What else was there for me to do? We had no money. No man was going to come and take me away. I didn't want to rot in that country." As though she wasn't rotting now.'

Willie said, 'I understand your friend. I wanted to be a priest at one time. And a missionary. I wanted to be like the fathers. They were so much better off than the people around us. There seemed to be no other way out.' And the thought came to him that Ana's situation in her country might be something like his at home.

At another time on the little sofa Ana said, 'Here's a story for your next book. If you think you can do anything with it. My mother had a friend called Luisa. Nobody knew anything about Luisa's parentage. She had been adopted by a rich estate-owning family and she inherited a part of the estate. Luisa went to Portugal and Europe. She lived extravagantly for many years and then she announced she had found a wonderful man. She brought him back. They gave a very big party in the capital, and the wonderful man told everybody about all the famous people who were his close friends in Europe. After that he and Luisa went out to the bush, to live on Luisa's estate. People were expecting the great friends to come out, the big house to be opened up. But nothing happened. Luisa and her wonderful man just grew fat, telling the same stories they had told at the time of their party. Fewer and fewer people went to see them. After a time the man began to sleep with African women, but even that became too much for him, and he gave up. So Luisa the adopted child and her wonderful man lived happily or unhappily and then died, and Luisa's family fortune vanished, and nobody knew who Luisa was or who the wonderful man was. That's how my mother used to tell the story. And here's another story. There was this dowdy and unhappy girl at the boarding school. She was living in the bush somewhere with her father and stepmother. Then the girl's real mother marries again, and the girl goes to live with her. The girl changes in a remarkable way. She becomes stylish, happy, a glamour girl. Her happiness doesn't last long. Her stepfather becomes interested in her, too interested. He goes into the girl's bedroom one night. There is a scene, and then a divorce and a great scandal.'

And Willie knew that the girl in that second story, the unhappy girl in the frightening, destructive bush of her African country, was Ana. He thought it explained her thinness, her nervousness. It increased his feeling for her.

A letter came from Sarojini in Cuba, with a photograph. *This man says he knows you. He is a Latin American from Panama and his name is Cato, because his family has spent much time in the British colonies. He says that in the old days people gave their slaves Greek and Roman names as a joke, and his ancestor was landed with the name of Cato. He is off now to work with Che in South America, where there is so much to do, and one day perhaps he will be able to go back to Jamaica to do some work there. That's where his heart is. He should be an example to you.*

In the square black-and-white photograph, which was not well focused, Percy was sitting on a half-wall, legs dangling, in the slanting light of morning or late afternoon. He was wearing a striped woollen cap and a whitish tunic or bush shirt with a raised embroidered design in the same whitish colour. So he was as stylish as ever. He was smiling at the camera, and in his bright eyes Willie thought he could see all the other Percies: the Percies of Jamaica and Panama, Notting Hill and the bohemian parties, and the college of education.

What are your plans? We get very little news of England here, just a little item from time to time about the race riots. Was your book published? You kept it to yourself. You didn't send us a copy, and I suppose it's come and gone. Well, now that you've got it out of your system, it's time for you to put that kind of vanity aside, and think more constructively about the future.

Willie thought, 'She's right. I've been believing in magic. My time's nearly finished here. My scholarship is nearly at an end, and I have planned nothing at all. I've been living here in a fool's paradise. When my time is up and they throw me out of the college, my life is going to change completely. I will have to look for a place to stay. I will have to look for a job. It will be a different London then. Ana wouldn't want to come to a room in Notting Hill. I am going to lose her.'

He worried like this for some days and then he thought, 'I've been a fool. I've been waiting to be guided to where I should go. Waiting for a sign. And all this time the sign's been there. I must go with Ana to her country.'

When they next met he said, 'Ana, I would like to go with you to Africa.'

'For a holiday?'

'For good.'

She said nothing. A week or so later he said, 'You

remember what I said about going to Africa?' Her face clouded. He said, 'You've read my stories. You know I've nowhere else to go. And I don't want to lose you.' She looked confused. He didn't say any more. Later, when she was leaving, she said, 'You must give me time. I have to think.' When she next came to his room, and they were on the little sofa, she said, 'Do you think you'll like Africa?'

He said, 'You think there'll be something I'll be able to do there?'

'Let's see how you like the bush. We need a man on the estate. But you'll have to learn the language.'

In his last week at the college a letter came from Sarojini in Colombia. *I am glad you've at last got the diploma, though I don't know what you will do with it where you are going. Serious work has to be done in Africa, especially in those Portuguese places, but I don't think it will be done by you. You are like your father, holding on to old ideas till the end. About other matters, I hope you know what you are doing, Willie. I don't understand what you write about the girl. Outsiders who go to India have no idea of the country even when they are there, and I am sure the same is true of Africa. Please be careful. You are putting yourself in the hands of strangers. You think you know what you are going to, but you don't know all of it.*

Willie thought, 'She likes her own international marriage, but she is worried about mine.'

But, as always, her words, glib though they were, the words of someone still mimicking adulthood, troubled him and stayed with him. He heard them as he did his packing, removing his presence bit by bit from the college room, undoing the centre of his London life. Undoing that, so easily now, he wondered how he would ever set about getting a footing in the city again if at some time he had to. He might have luck again; there might be something like the chain of chance encounters he had had; but they would lead him into a city he didn't know.

* * *

THEY – HE AND ANA – left from Southampton. He thought about the new language he would have to learn. He wondered whether he would be able to hold on to his own language. He wondered whether he would forget his English, the language of his stories. He set himself little tests, and when one test was over he immediately started on another. While the Mediterranean went by, and the other passengers lunched and dined and played shipboard games, Willie was trying to deal with the knowledge that had come to him on the ship that his home language had almost gone, that his English was going, that he had no proper language left, no gift of expression. He didn't tell Ana. Every time he spoke he was testing himself, to see how much he still knew, and he preferred to stay in the cabin dealing with this foolish thing that had befallen him. Alexandria was spoilt for him, and the Suez Canal. (He remembered – as from another, happier life, far from his passage now between the red desert glare on both sides – Krishna Menon in his dark double-breasted suit walking beside the flowerbeds in Hyde Park, leaning on his stick, looking down, working out his United Nations speech about Egypt and the Canal.)

Three years before, when he was going to England, he

had done this part of the journey in the opposite direction. He hardly knew then what he was seeing. He had a better idea now of geography and history; he had some idea of the antiquity of Egypt. He would have liked to commit the landscape to memory, but his worry about the loss of language kept him from concentrating. It was in the same unsatisfactory way that he saw the coast of Africa: Port Sudan, on the edge of an immense desolation; Djibouti; and then, past the Horn of Africa, Mombasa, Dar-es-Salaam, and finally the port of Ana's country. All this while he had been acting reasonably and lucidly. Neither Ana nor anyone else would have known that there was anything wrong. But all this while Willie felt that there was another self inside him, in a silent space where all his external life was muffled.

He wished he had come to Ana's country in another way. The town was big and splendid, far finer than anything he had imagined, not something he would have associated with Africa. Its grandeur worried him. He didn't think he would be able to cope with it. The strange people he saw on the streets knew the language and the ways of the place. He thought, 'I am not staying here. I am leaving. I will spend a few nights here and then I will find some way of going away.' That was how he thought all the time he was in the capital, in the house of one of Ana's friends, and that was how he thought during the slow further journey in a small coasting ship to the northern province where the estate was: going back a small part of the way he had just come, but closer now to the land, closer to the frightening mouths and wetlands of very wide rivers, quiet and empty, mud and water mixing in great slow swirls of green and brown. Those were the rivers that barred any road or land route to the north.

They got off at last at a little low-built concrete town, grey and ochre and fading white, with straight streets like the capital but without big advertisements, without even that clue to the life of the place. Just outside, the narrow asphalt road led inland through open country. Always, then, Africans, small and slight people here, walking on the red earth on either side of the asphalt, walking as if in wilderness, but it was not wilderness to them. Never far away, marked by scratchings of maize and cassava and other things, were African settlements, huts and reed-fenced yards, the huts with straight neat lines and roofs of a long fine grass that seemed at times to catch the sun and then shone like long, well-brushed hair. Very big grey rocks, cone-shaped, some the size of hills, rose abruptly out of the earth, each rock cone isolated, a landmark on its own. They turned off into a dirt road. The bush was as high as the car and the villages they passed were more crowded than on the asphalt road. The dirt road was red and dry but there were old puddles that splashed spots of black mud on the windscreen. They left this road and began to climb a noticeable slope towards the house. The road here was corrugated when straight; where it turned it was trenched by the rains, water making its own way down. The house was in the middle of an overgrown old garden and in the shade of a great, branching rain tree. Bougainvillaea screened the verandah which ran on three sides of the lower floor.

The air was hot and stale inside. Looking out from the bedroom window, through wire netting and dead insects, at the rough garden and the tall paw-paw trees and the land falling away past groves of cashews and clusters of grass roofs to the rock cones which in the distance appeared to make a continuous low pale-blue range, Willie thought, 'I don't know where I am. I don't think I can pick my way back. I don't ever want this view to become familiar. I must not unpack. I must never behave as though I am staying.'

He stayed for eighteen years.

He slipped one day on the front steps of the estate house. Ana's white grandfather, who at one time went every year to Lisbon and Paris – that was the story – had built the house in the early days of money, after the 1914 war, and the front steps were semi-circular and of imported white-and-grey marble. The marble was now cracked, mossy in the cracks, and on this rainy morning slippery with the wet and the pollen from the big shade tree.

Willie woke up in the military hospital in the town. He was among wounded black soldiers with shining faces and tired red eyes. When Ana came to see him he said, 'I am going to leave you.'

She said, in the voice that had enchanted him, and which he still liked, 'You've had a nasty fall. I've told that new girl so often to sweep the steps. That marble has always been slippery. Especially after rain. Foolish, really, for a place like this.'

'I am going to leave you.'

'You slipped, Willie. You were unconscious for some time. People exaggerate the fighting in the bush. You know that. There's not going to be a new war.'

'I'm not thinking of the fighting. The world is full of slippery substances.'

She said, 'I'll come back later.'

When she came back, he said, 'Do you think that it would be possible for someone to look at all my bruises and cuts and work out what had happened to me? Work out what I have done to myself?'

'You're recovering your spirits.'

'You've had eighteen years of me.'

'You really mean that you are tired of me.'

'I mean I've given you eighteen years. I can't give you any more. I can't live your life any more. I want to live my own.'

'It was your idea, Willie. And if you leave, where will you go?'

'I don't know. But I must stop living your life here.'

When she left he called the mulatto matron and, very slowly, spelling out the English words, he dictated a letter to Sarojini. For years, for just such a situation, he had always memorised Sarojini's address – in Colombia, Jamaica, Bolivia, Peru, Argentina, Jordan, and half a dozen other countries – and now, even more slowly, for he was uncertain himself about the German words – he dictated an address in West Berlin to the matron. He gave her one of the old English five-pound notes Ana had brought for him, and later that day the matron took the letter and the money to the almost stripped shop of an Indian merchant, one of the few merchants left in the town. There was no proper postal service since the Portuguese had left and the guerrillas had taken over. But this merchant, who had contacts all along the eastern African coast, could get things onto local sailing craft going north, to Dar-es-Salaam and Mombasa. There the letters could be stamped and sent on.

The letter, awkwardly addressed, passed from hand to hand in Africa, and then awkwardly stamped, came one day in a small red mail-cart to its destination in Charlottenburg. And six weeks later Willie himself was there. Old snow lay on the pavements, with paths of yellow sand and salt in the middle, and scatterings of dog dirt on the snow. Sarojini lived in a big, dark flat up two flights of stairs. Wolf wasn't there. Willie hadn't met him and wasn't looking forward to meeting him. Sarojini said simply, 'He's with his other family.' And Willie was happy to leave it like that, to probe no further.

The flat seemed to have been neglected for years, and it made Willie think, with a sinking heart, of the estate house he had just left. Sarojini said, 'It hasn't been decorated since before the war.' The paint was old and smoky, many layers thick, one pale colour upon another, with decorative details on plaster and wood clogged up, and in many places the old paint layers had chipped through to dark old wood. But while Ana's house was full of her family's heavy furniture, Sarojini's big flat was half empty. The few pieces of furniture were basic and second-hand and seemed to have been chosen with no particular care. The plates and cups and knives and spoons were all cheap. Everything had a makeshift air. It was no pleasure at all to Willie to eat the food Sarojini cooked in the small stale-smelling kitchen at the back.

She had given up the style of sari and cardigan and socks. She was in jeans and a heavy sweater and her manner was brisker and even more authoritative than Willie remembered. Willie thought, 'All of this was buried in the girl I had left behind at home. None of this would have come out if the German hadn't come and taken her away. If he hadn't come, would she and all her soul have just rotted to nothing?' She was attractive now – something impossible to think of in the ashram days – and gradually from things she said or let drop Willie understood that she had had many lovers since he had last seen her.

Within days of coming to Berlin he had begun to lean on this strength of his sister. After Africa, he liked the idea of the great cold, and she took him out walking, treacherous though the pavements were, and shaky though he still was. Sometimes when they were in restaurants Tamil boys came in selling long-stalked roses. They were unsmiling, boys with a mission, raising funds for the great Tamil war far away, and they hardly looked at Willie or his sister. They were of another generation, but Willie saw himself in them. He thought, 'That was how I appeared in London. That is how I appear now. I am not as alone as I thought.' Then he thought, 'But I am wrong. I am not like them. I am forty-one, in middle life. They are fifteen or twenty years younger, and the world has changed. They have proclaimed who they are and they are risking everything for it. I have been hiding from myself. I have risked nothing. And now the best part of my life is over.'

Sometimes in the evenings they saw Africans in the blue light of telephone kiosks pretending to talk, but really just occupying space, taking a kind of shelter. Sarojini said, 'The East Germans fly them into East Berlin, and then they come here.' Willie thought, 'How many of us there now are! How many like me! Can there be room for us all?'

He asked Sarojini, 'What happened to my friend Percy Cato? You wrote about him a long time ago.'

Sarojini said, 'He was doing well with Che and the others. Then some kind of rage possessed him. He had left Panama as a child and he had a child's idea of the continent. When he went back he began to see the place differently. He became full of hatred for the Spaniards. You could say he reached the Pol Pot position.'

Willie said, 'What is the Pol Pot position?'

'He thought the Spaniards had raped and looted the continent in the most savage way, and no good could come out of the place until all the Spaniards or part-Spaniards were killed. Until that happened revolution itself was a waste of time. It is a difficult idea, but actually it's interesting, and liberation movements will have to take it on board some day. Latin America can break your heart. But Percy didn't know how to present his ideas, and he could forget he was working with Spaniards. He could have been more tactful. I don't think he cared to explain himself too much. They eased him out. Behind his back they began calling him the *negrito*. In the end he went back to Jamaica. The word was that he was working for the revolution there, but then we found out that he was running a night-club for tourists on the north coast.'

Willie said, 'He wasn't a drinking man, but his heart was always in that work. Being smooth with the smooth and rough with the rough.'

And just as once his father had told Willie about his life, so now, over many days of the Berlin winter, in cafés and restaurants and the half-empty flat, Willie began slowly to tell Sarojini of his life in Africa.

* * *

THE FIRST DAY AT Ana's estate house (Willie said) was as long as you can imagine. Everything in the house – the colours, the wood, the furniture, the smells – was new to me. Everything in the bathroom was new to me – all the slightly antiquated fittings, and the old geyser for heating water. Other people had designed that room, had had those fittings installed, had chosen those white wall tiles – some of them cracked now, the crack-lines and the grouting black with mould or dirt, the walls themselves a little uneven. Other people had become familiar with all those things, had considered them part of the comfort of the house. In that room especially I felt a stranger.

Somehow I got through the day, without Ana or anyone else guessing at my state of mind, the profound doubt that had been with me ever since we had left England. And then it was night. A generator came on. The power it provided went up and down. The bulbs all over the house and the outbuildings constantly dimmed and brightened, and the light they gave seemed to answer a pulse beat, now filling a room, now shrinking back to the walls. I waited all the time that first night for the light to steady itself. At about ten the lights dipped very low. Some minutes later they dipped again, and a while after that they went out. The generator whined down and I was aware of the noise it had been making. There was a ringing in my ears, then something like the sound of crickets in the night, then silence and the dark, the two coming together. Afterwards the pale yellow lights of oil lamps could be seen in the servants' quarters at the back of the house.

I felt very far away from everything I had known, a stranger in that white concrete house with all the strange old Portuguese colonial furniture, the unfamiliar old bathroom fittings; and when I lay down to sleep I saw again – for longer than I had seen them that day – the fantastic rock cones, the straight asphalt road, and the Africans walking.

I drew comfort from Ana, her strength and her authority. And just as now, as you may have noticed, Sarojini, I lean on you, so in those days, ever since she had agreed to my being with her in Africa, I leaned on Ana. I believed in a special way in her luck. Some of this had to do with the very fact that she was a woman who had given herself to me. I believed that she was in some essential way guided and protected, and as long as I was with her no harm could come to me. It may be because of something in our culture that, in spite of appearances, men are really looking for women to lean on. And, of course, if you are not used to governments or the law or society or even history being on your side, then you have to believe in your luck or your star or you will die. I know that you have inherited our mother's uncle's radical genes and have different ideas. I am not going to argue with you. I just want to tell you why I was able to follow someone I hardly knew to a colonial country in Africa of which I knew little except that it had difficult racial and social ideas. I loved Ana and I believed in her luck. The two ideas went together. And since I know, Sarojini, that you have your own ideas about love as well, I will explain. Ana was important to me because I depended on her for my idea of being a man. You know what I mean and I think we can call it love. So I loved Ana, for the great gift she had brought me, and to an equal degree I believed in her luck. I would have gone anywhere with her.

In the sitting room one morning, in that first or second week, I found a little African maid. She was very thin, shiny-faced, and in a flimsy cotton dress. She said, in an overfamiliar but rather stylish way, 'So you are Ana's London man.' She put her broom against the high upholstered armchair, sat on the chair as on a throne, both her forearms resting flat on the worn upholstered arms of the chair, and began to engage me in polite conversation. She said, as if speaking from a textbook, 'Did you have a pleasant journey?' And: 'Have you had a chance to see something of the country? What do you think of the country?' I had been studying the language for some time and knew enough of it now to talk in the same stilted way to the little maid. Ana came in. She said, 'I wondered who it was.' The little maid dropped her grand manner, got up from the chair and took up her broom again. Ana said, 'Her father is Júlio. He is the carpenter. He drinks too much.'

I had met Júlio. He was a man of mixed race with smiling unreliable eyes, and he lived in the servants' quarters. His drinking was a joke there, and I was to learn not to be too frightened by it. He was a weekend drinker, and often late in the afternoon on a Friday or Saturday or Sunday his African wife would run out to the garden of the main house, quite alone in her terror, moving backwards or sideways step by step, her African cloth slipping off her shoulder, watching all the time for the drunken man in the quarters. This could go on until the light faded. Then the generator would come on, drowning everything with its vibration. The unsteady electric light would further alter the aspect of things; the crisis would pass; and in the quarters in the morning there would be peace again, the passions of the evening washed away.

But it couldn't have been much of a joke for Júlio's daughter. She spoke in her simple and open way of her home life, in those two rooms at the back. She said to me, 'When my father gets drunk he beats my mother. Sometimes he beats me too. Sometimes it's so bad I can't sleep. Then I walk up and down the room until I get tired. Sometimes I walk all night.' And every night after that, whenever I got into bed, I thought for a second or two about the little maid in the quarters. Another time she said to me, 'We eat the same food every day.' I didn't know whether she was complaining or boasting or simply speaking a fact about her African ways. In those early days, until local people made me think differently about African girls, I used to worry about Júlio's daughter, seeing myself in her, and wondering how, with all her feelings for fineness as I saw them, she was going to manage in the wilderness in which she found herself.

Of course it wasn't wilderness. It looked open and wild, but it had all been charted and parcelled out, and every thirty minutes or so on those dirt roads, if you were driving in a suitable vehicle, you came to an estate house which was more or less like Ana's. Something in newish white concrete with a wide, bougainvillaea-hung verandah all around, and with additions at the back.

We went one Sunday, not long after we had arrived, to a

lunch at one of those neighbours of Ana's. It was a big affair. There were mud-splashed Jeeps and Land-Rovers and other four-wheel drives on the sandy open space in front of the house. The African servants wore white uniforms, buttoned at the neck. After drinks people separated according to their inclination, some sitting at the big table in the dining room, others sitting at the smaller tables on the verandah, where the tangled old bougainvillaea vines softened the light. I had had no idea what these people would be like and what they would think of me. Ana hadn't talked of the matter and, following her example, I hadn't talked of it to her. I found now that there was no special reaction to me. It was curiously deflating. I was expecting some recognition of my extraordinariness and there was nothing. Some of these estate-owners appeared, in fact, to have no conversation; it was as though the solitude of their lives had taken away that faculty. When eating time came they just sat and ate, husband and wife side by side, not young, not old, people in between in age, eating and not talking, not looking round, very private, as though they were in their own houses. Towards the end of the lunch two or three of these eating women beckoned the servants and talked to them, and after a while the servants came with take-away portions of the lunch in paper bags. It appeared to be a tradition of the place. It might have been that they had come from far, and wanted to have food to eat when they got back home.

Racially they were varied, from what looked like pure white to a deep brown. A number of them were of my father's complexion, and this might have been one reason why they seemed to accept me. Ana said later, 'They don't know what

to make of you.' There were Indians in the country; I wasn't
an absolute exotic. There were quite a few Indian traders.
They ran cheap shops and socially never stepped outside their
families. There was an old and large Goan community, people
originally of India, from the very old Portuguese colony
there, who had come to this place in Africa to work as clerks
and accountants in the civil service. They spoke Portuguese
with a special accent. I couldn't be mistaken for a Goan.
My Portuguese was poor and for some reason I spoke it with
an English accent. So people couldn't place me and they let
me be. I was Ana's London man, as the little housemaid had
said.

About the people at the lunch Ana told me afterwards,
'They are the second-rank Portuguese. That is how they are
considered officially, and that is how they consider themselves.
They are second rank because most of them have an African
grandparent, like me.' In those days to be even a second-rank
Portuguese was to have a kind of high status, and just as at
the lunch they kept their heads down and ate, so in the
colonial state they kept their heads down and made what
money they could. That was to change in a couple of years,
but at the moment that regulated colonial world seemed rock
solid to everybody. And that was the world in which, for the
first time, I found a complete acceptance.

Those were the days of my intensest love-making with
Ana. I loved her – in that room that had been her grandfather's and her mother's, with a view of the nervous
branching and the fine leaves of the rain tree – for the luck
and liberation she had brought me, the undoing of fear,
the granting to me of full manhood. I loved, as always, the

seriousness of her face at those moments. There was a little curl to her hair just as it sprang out of her temples. In that curl I saw her African ancestry, and loved her for that too. And one day I realised that for all of the past week I had not thought about my fear of losing language and expression, the fear almost of losing the gift of speech.

The estate grew cotton and cashews and sisal. I knew nothing about these crops. But there was a manager and there were overseers. They lived about ten minutes away from the main house, down their own little dirt road, in a cluster of similar little white concrete bungalows with corrugated-iron roofs and small verandahs. Ana had said that the estate needed a man, and I knew, without being told, that my only function was to reinforce Ana's authority with these men. I never tried to do more than that, and the overseers accepted me. I knew that in accepting me they were really respecting Ana's authority. So we all got on. I began to learn. I took pleasure in a way of life that was far from anything I had known or envisaged for myself.

I used to worry in the beginning about the overseers. They didn't seem to have much of a life. They were mixed-race people, born in the country most of them, and they lived in that row of small concrete houses. Only the concrete of their houses separated the overseers from the Africans all around. African thatch and wattle was ordinary; concrete stood for dignity. But concrete wasn't a true barrier. These overseers lived, really, with the Africans. No other way was open to them. I used to think, trying to put myself in their place, that with their mixed background they might have felt the need of something more. There was the town on the coast. It offered a different kind of life, but it was more than an hour away in daylight and a good deal more after dark. It was a place only for quick excursions. To work on the estate was to live on the estate, and it was known that many of the overseers had African families. Whatever face these men showed us, the life waiting for them at home, in their concrete houses, was an African life at which I could only guess.

One day, when I was driving with one of the overseers to a new cotton field, I began to talk to the man about his life. We were in a Land-Rover, and we had left the dirt road and were driving through bush, avoiding the bigger boggy dips and the dead branches of felled trees. I was expecting to hear some story of unfulfilled ambition from the overseer, some story of things going wrong, expecting to catch some little resentment of people better off and in the world outside. But there was no resentment. The overseer thought himself blessed. He had tried living in Portugal; he had even tried living in a South African town; he had come back. He hit the steering wheel of the Land-Rover with the heel of his palm and said, 'I can't live anywhere else.' When I asked why, he said, 'This. What we are doing now. You can't do this in Portugal.' Land-Rovers and four-wheel drives were new to me; I was still excited myself to drive off a road and pick a way through hummocky wet bush. But I felt that the overseer had a larger appreciation of the life of the place; his surrender was more than the simple sexual thing it seemed. And when I next saw the mildewed white staff bungalows I looked at them with a new respect. So bit by bit I learned. Not only about cotton and sisal and cashew, but also about the people.

I got used to the road to the town. I knew the giant rock cones along the way. Each cone had its own shape and was a marker for me. Some cones rose clean out of the ground; some had a rock debris at their base where a face of the cone had flaked off; some cones were grey and bare; some had a yellowish lichen on one side; on the ledges of some which had flaked there was vegetation, sometimes even a tree. The cones were always new. It was always an adventure, after a week or two on the estate, to drive to the town. For an hour or so it always seemed new: the colonial shops, the rustic, jumbled shop windows, the African loaders sitting outside the shops waiting for a loading job; the paved streets, the cars and trucks, the garages; the mixed population, with the red-faced young Portuguese conscripts of our little garrison giving a strange air of Europe to the place. The garrison was as yet very small; and the barracks were still small and plain and unthreatening, low two-storey buildings in white or grey concrete, of a piece with the rest of the town. Sometimes there was a new café to go to. But cafés didn't last in our town. The conscripts didn't have money, and the townspeople preferred to live privately.

Most of the shops we used were Portuguese. One or two were Indian. I was nervous of going into them at first. I didn't want to get that look from the shop people that would remind me of home and bad things. But there was never anything like that, no flicker of racial recognition from the family inside. There, too, they accepted the new person I had become in Ana's country. They seemed not to know that I was once something else. There, too, they kept their heads down and did what they had to do. So that for me, as for the overseers, though in different ways, the place offered an extra little liberation.

Sometimes on a weekend we went to the beach beyond the town, and a rough little Portuguese weekend restaurant serving fish and shellfish plucked fresh from the sea, and red and white Portuguese wine.

I often thought back to the terror of my first day – that picture of the road and the Africans walking was always with me – and wondered that the land had been tamed in this way, that such a reasonable life could be extracted from such an unpromising landscape, that blood, in some way, had been squeezed out of stone.

It would have been different sixty or seventy years before, when Ana's grandfather had arrived to take over the immense tract of land he had been granted by a government that felt its own weakness and was anxious – in the face of the restless power and greater populations of Britain and Germany – to occupy the African colony it claimed. The town would have been the roughest little coastal settlement with a population of black Arabs, people produced by a century and more of racial mixing. The road inland would have been a dirt track. Everything would have been transported by cart at two miles an hour. The journey I did now in an hour would have taken two days. The estate house would have been very simple, not too different from the African huts, but done with timber and corrugated iron and nails and metal hinges, everything sent up by ship from the capital and then put into carts. There would have been no electric light, no wire-netting screen against mosquitoes, no water except the rain-water that ran off the roof. To live there would have been to live with the land, month after month, year after year, to live with the climate and diseases, and to depend completely on the people. It was not easy to imagine. Just as no man can truly wish to be somebody else, since no man can imagine himself without the heart and mind he has been granted, so no man of a later time can really know what it was like to live on the land in those days. We can judge only by what we know. Ana's grandfather, and all the people he knew, would have known only what they had. They would have been content to live with that.

All down the coast, the Arabs of Muscat and Oman, the previous settlers, had become fully African. They had ceased to be Arabs and were known locally only as Mohammedans. Ana's grandfather, living that hard life in that hard country, and knowing no other, had himself become half-African, with an African family. But while for the African Arabs of the coast history had not moved for generations, and they had been allowed to stay what they had become, history began unexpectedly to quicken around Ana's grandfather. There was the great 1914 war in Europe. Ana's grandfather made a fortune then. More settlers came out to the country; the capital developed; there were trams, with white people (and Goans) at the front and Africans at the back, behind a canvas barrier. Ana's grandfather wished, in this period, to recover the European personality he had shed. He sent his two half-African daughters to Europe to be educated; it was no secret that he wished them to marry Portuguese. And he built his big estate house, with white concrete walls and red concrete floors. There was a big garden at the front and side, and a line of verandahed guest rooms running off the main verandah at the back. Each guest room had its own big bathroom with the fittings of the day. The servants' quarters were extensive; they were at the very back. He bought the fine colonial furniture that was still around us. We slept in his bedroom, Ana and I, on his high carved bed. If it was hard to enter the personality of the man who had become half-African, it was harder to be at ease with this later personality, which should have been more approachable. I always felt a stranger in the house. I never got used to the grandeur; the furniture seemed strange and awkward right to the end.

And, with my background, always in such a situation scratching at me, I couldn't forget the Africans. Ana's grand-father, and the others, and the priests and nuns of the frightening pretty foreign mission, old-fashioned in style, that had been set down, just like that, in the open, bare land, all of these people would have thought the right thing was to bend Africans to their will, to fit them for the new way. I wondered how they had set about that, and was afraid to ask. Yet somehow the Africans had stayed themselves, with many of their traditions and much of their own religion, though the land around them had been parcelled out and planted with crops they were required to tend. Those people walking on either side of the asphalt road were much more than estate labour. They had social obligations which were as intricate as those I knew at home. They could without warning take days off estate work and walk long distances to pay a cere-monial call or take a gift to someone. When they walked they didn't stop to drink water; they appeared not to need it. In the matter of eating and drinking they still at that time followed their own old ways. They drank water at the beginning of the day and then at the end, never in between. They ate nothing at the beginning of the day, before they went out to work; and the first meal they had, in the middle of the morning, was of vegetables alone. They ate their own kind of food, and most of what they ate was grown in the mixed planting just around their huts. Dried cassava was the staple. It could be ground into flour or eaten as it was. Two or three sticks of it could keep a man going all day when he went on a journey. In the smallest village you could see people selling dried cassava from their little crop, a sack or two at a time, gambling with their own need in the weeks to come.

It was strange when you got to see it, those two different worlds side by side: the big estates and the concrete buildings, and the African world that seemed less consequential but was everywhere, like a kind of sea. It was like a version of what – in another life, as it seemed – I had known at home.

By a strange chance I was on the other side here. But I used to think, when I got to know more of the story, that Ana's grandfather wouldn't have liked it if he had been told at the end of his life that someone like me was going to live in his estate house and sit in his fine chairs and sleep with his granddaughter in his big carved bed. He had had quite another idea of the future of his family and his name. He had sent his two half-African daughters to school in Portugal, and everyone knew that he wanted them to marry proper Portuguese, to breed out the African inheritance he had given them in the hard days when he had lived very close to the land with less and less idea of another world outside.

The girls were pretty and they had money. It was no trouble for them, especially during the great Depression, to find husbands in Portugal. One girl stayed in Portugal. The other, Ana's mother, came back to Africa and the estate with her husband. There were lunches, parties, visits. Ana's grandfather couldn't show off his son-in-law enough. He gave up his bedroom, with its extravagant furniture, to the couple. So as not to be in the way, he moved to one of the guest rooms at the rear of the main building; and then, out of a greater tact, he moved to one of the overseers' houses some distance away. After some time Ana was born. And then, little by little, in that bedroom to which I woke up every morning, Ana's father became very strange. He became listless and passive. He had no duties on the estate, nothing to rouse him, and some days he never left the room, never left the bed. The story among the mixed-race overseers, and our neighbours – and, inevitably, it got to me not long after I arrived – was that the marriage that had looked good to Ana's father in Portugal looked less good in Africa, and he had become full of resentment.

Ana knew the stories that were told about her father. She said, when we began to talk about these things, 'It was true, what they said. But it was only part of the truth. I suppose when he was in Portugal he thought, apart from everything else, apart from the money, I mean, that it would help him, going out in a privileged way to the new country. But he wasn't made for the bush. He was never an active man, and his energy level fell when he came here. The less he did, the more he hid in his room, the lower his energy fell. He felt no anger for me or my mother or my grandfather. He was just passive. He hated being asked to do very simple things. I remember how his face would twist with pain and anger.

He really was someone who needed help. As a child I thought of him as a sick man and his bedroom as a sickroom. It made my childhood here very unhappy. As a child I used to think, about my father and my mother, 'These people don't know that I'm a person, too, that I too need help. I'm not a toy they just happened to make.'

In time Ana's parents began to live separate lives. Her mother lived in the family house in the capital, looking after Ana while she was at the convent school there. And for many years no one outside the family knew that anything was wrong. It was the pattern in colonial days: the wife in the capital or one of the coastal towns looking after the education of the children, the husband looking after the estate. Usually, because of this repeated separation, husbands began to live with African women and have African families. But the other thing happened here: Ana's mother took a lover in the capital, a mixed-race man, a civil servant, high up in the customs, but still only a civil servant. The affair went on and on. It became common knowledge. Ana's grandfather, near the end of his life now, felt mocked. He blamed Ana's mother for the bad marriage and everything else. He felt her African blood had taken over. Just before he died he changed his will. He gave to Ana what he had intended to give to her mother.

Ana was now at a language school in England. She said, 'I wanted to break out of the Portuguese language. I feel it was that that had made my grandfather such a limited man. He had no true idea of the world. All he could think of was Portugal and Portuguese Africa and Goa and Brazil. In his mind, because of the Portuguese language, all the rest of the world had been strained away. And I didn't want to learn

South African English, which is what people learn here. I wanted to learn English English.'

It was while she was at the language school in Oxford that her father disappeared. He left the estate house one day and never came back. And he had taken a fair amount of the estate with him. He had used some legal loophole and had mortgaged away half of Ana's estate, including the family house in the capital. There was no question of Ana paying back the money he had raised; so everything that was mortgaged to the banks went to the banks. It was as though the overseers and everybody else who for more than twenty years had doubted her father had in the end been proved right. That was when she had called her mother and her lover to live on the estate. She joined them after the language school, and there had been happy times until one night the lover had tried to get into the big carved bed with her.

She said, 'But I told you that in London, in a disguised way.'

She still loved her father. She said, 'I suppose he always knew what he was doing. I suppose he always had some kind of plan like that. It would have taken a lot of planning, what he did. There would have been many trips to the capital, and many meetings with lawyers and the banks. But his illness was also real. The low energy, the helplessness. And he loved me. I never doubted that. Just before I met you I went to see him in Portugal. That was where he ended up. He had tried South Africa first, but that was too hard for him. He didn't like doing everything in a foreign language. He could have gone to Brazil, but he was too frightened. So he went back to Portugal. He was living in Coimbra. In a little flat in a modern block. Nothing too grand. But he was still living off the mortgage money. So in a way you could say he had struck gold. He was living alone. There was no sign of a woman's hand in the flat. It was all so sparse and bare it clutched at my heart. He was very affectionate, but in a dead kind of way. At one stage he asked me to go to the bedroom to get some medicine for him from his bedside table, and when I went and opened the drawer I saw an old Kodak 620 snapshot of myself as a girl. I thought I was going to break down. But then I thought, 'He's planned this.' I pulled myself together, and when I went back to him I was careful to let nothing show on my face. He called one of the two bedrooms his studio. I was puzzled by that, but it turned out that he had begun to do little modern sculptures in bronze, little figures of half-horses and half-birds and half-other things, one side green and rough, one side highly polished. I actually loved what he did. He said it took him two or three months to do a piece. He gave me a little hawk he'd done. I put it in my bag and every day I would take it out and hold it, feeling the shine and the rough. I actually thought for two or three weeks that he was an artist, and I was very proud. I thought that he had done everything he had done because he was an artist. Then I began to see bronze pieces like his everywhere. It was souvenir stuff. The work he was doing in his studio was part of his idleness. I felt ashamed of myself, for thinking that he might have been an artist, and for not pressing him more. Asking the questions I should have asked him. That was just before I met you. I think you will see now why your stories spoke to me. All the bluff, the make-believe, with the real unhappiness. It was uncanny. It was why I wrote.'

She had never been so explicit about the stories, and it worried me to think that I might have given away more of myself than I knew, and that she had probably always known who and what I was. I didn't have a copy of the book; I had wished to leave all that behind. Ana still had her copy. But I was unwilling to look at it, nervous of what I might find.

I had brought very little with me in the way of papers. I had two exercise books with stories and sketches I had done at the mission school at home. I had some letters of Roger's in his lovely educated handwriting; for some reason I hadn't wanted to throw them away. And I had my Indian passport and two five-pound notes. I thought of that as my get-away money. Ana had taken me as a pauper, and it was as though from the very beginning I knew I would one day have to leave. Ten pounds wouldn't have got me far; but it was all the spare money I had in London; and in the corner of my mind where with some kind of ancestral caution I had made this half-plan or quarter-plan I thought it would at least get me started. The ten pounds and the passport and the other things were in an old brown envelope in the bottom drawer of a heavy bureau in the bedroom.

One day I couldn't find that envelope. I asked the house people; Ana asked. But no one had seen anything or had anything to say. The loss of the passport worried me more than everything else. Without my passport I didn't see how I could prove to any official in Africa or England or India who I was. It was all right for Ana to say that I should write home for another passport. Her idea of bureaucracy was of a strict, impartial thing, grinding slowly, but grinding. I knew the ways of our offices — easy for me to re-create in my mind's eye: the pea-green walls shiny with grime at the levels of head and shoulders and bottom, the rough carpentry of counters and cashiers' cages, the floor black with dirt, the *pan*-chewing clerks in their trousers or *lungis*, each man correctly marked on the forehead with a fresh caste-mark (his principal duty of the day), on every desk the ragged stacks of old files in many faded colours, poor-quality paper crumbling away – and I knew that I would wait a long time in far-off Africa, and nothing would come. Without my passport I had no credentials, no claim on anyone. I would be lost. I wouldn't be able to move. The more I thought about it, the more unprotected I felt. For some days I could think of nothing else. It began to be like my torment, on the way out, all down the coast of Africa, about losing the gift of language.

Ana said one morning, 'I've been talking to the cook. She thinks we should go to a fetish-man. There is a very famous one twenty or thirty miles from here. He is known in all the villages. I've asked the cook to call him.'

I said, 'Who do you think would want to steal a passport and old letters?'

Ana said, 'We mustn't spoil it now. We mustn't take any names. Please be ruled by me. We mustn't even think of anyone. We must leave it to the fetish-man. He's a very serious and self-respecting man.'

She said the next day, 'The fetish-man is coming in seven days.'

That day Júlio the carpenter found the brown envelope and one of Roger's letters in his workshop. Ana called the cook and said, 'That's good. But there are other things. The fetish-man still has to come.' Day after day it went on like this, with new discoveries – Roger's letters, my school exercise books – in various places. But the passport and the five-pound notes were still missing, and everyone knew that the fetish-man was still coming. In the end he never came. The day before he was due the passport and the money were found in one of the small drawers of the bureau. Ana sent the fetish-man money by the cook. He sent it back, because he hadn't come.

Ana said, 'It is something you must remember. Africans may not be afraid of you and me, but they are afraid of one another. Every man has access to the fetish-man, and this means that even the humblest man has power. In that way they are better off than the rest of us.'

I had got the passport back. I felt safe again. Ana and I, as if by agreement, talked no more about the matter. We never mentioned the fetish-man. But the ground had moved below me.

* * *

OUR FRIENDS – or the people we saw on weekends – had their estate houses within a two-hour drive. Most of that would have been on dirt roads, each with its own quirks and dangers (some roads twisting through African villages), and anything much beyond two hours was hard to do. The tropical day was twelve hours long, and the rule in the bush was that people on the road should try to get home by four and never later than five. Four hours' driving, with a three-hour lunch occasion in between, just about fitted into a Sunday; anything more was a test of stamina. So we saw the same people. I thought of them as Ana's friends; I never grew to think of them as my friends. And perhaps Ana had only inherited them with the estate. I suppose the friends could say that they had inherited us in the same way. We all came with the land.

In the beginning I saw this life as rich and exciting. I liked the houses, the very wide verandahs on all sides (hung with bougainvillaea or some other vine), the cool, dark inner rooms from where the bright light and the garden became beautiful – though the light was harsh when you were in it, full of stinging insects, and the garden was sandy and coarse, burnt away in some parts and in other parts threatening to go back to bush. From within these cool and comfortable houses the climate itself seemed like a blessing, as though the wealth of the people had brought about a change in nature, and the climate had ceased to be the punishing disease-laden thing it had been for Ana's grandfather and others in the early days.

In the beginning I wished only to be taken into this rich and safe life, so beyond anything I had imagined for myself, and I could be full of nerves when I met new people. I didn't want to see doubt in anyone's eyes. I didn't want questions I wouldn't be able to handle with Ana listening. But the questions were not asked; people kept whatever thoughts they might have had to themselves; among these estate people Ana had authority. And, very quickly, I shed my nerves. But then after a year or so I began to understand – and I was helped in this understanding by my own background – that the world I had entered was only a half-and-half world, that many of the people who were our friends considered themselves, deep down, people of the second rank.

They were not fully Portuguese, and that was where their own ambition lay.

With these half-and-half friends it was as with the town on the coast. It was always an adventure to drive to the town; but after an hour or so there everything went stale. In some such way a morning drive to an estate house for Sunday lunch could seem fresh and full of promise, but after an hour or so in the house with people who had lost their glamour, and whose stories were too well known, there was nothing more to say, and we were glad, all of us, to have the long business of eating and drinking to attend to, until, at three o'clock, when the sun was still high, we could get into our four-wheel drives and start for home.

These estate friends and neighbours, who had come with the land, we understood only in the broadest of ways. We saw them in the way they chose to present themselves to us; and we saw the same segment of the person each time. They became like people in a play we might have been studying at school, with everyone a 'character', and every character reduced to a few points.

The Correias, for instance, were proud of their aristocratic name. They were also obsessed with money. They talked about it all the time. They lived with the idea of a great disaster about to happen. They were not sure what this disaster was going to be, whether it was going to be local or worldwide, but they felt it was going to do away with their security both in Africa and Portugal. So they had bank accounts in London, New York and Switzerland. The idea was that when the bad time came they would have an 'envelope' of ready money in at least one of these places. The Correias spoke about these bank accounts to everybody. Sometimes they seemed simple-minded; sometimes they seemed to be boasting. But really what they wanted was to infect others with their vision of coming disaster, to start a little panic among their friends in the bush, if only to feel that in their own caution with the bank accounts they had been far-sighted, and ahead of everybody else.

Ricardo was a big, military-looking man with his grey hair in a military-style crewcut. He liked practising his English with me; he had a heavy South African accent. The big man lived with a great personal grief. His daughter had had promise as a singer. Everyone in the colony who heard her thought that she was special and had it in her to be a star in Europe. Ricardo, who was not a rich man, sold some land and sent the girl to Lisbon to be trained. There she had begun to live with an African from Angola, the Portuguese colony on the other side of the continent. It was the end of the girl's singing, the end of her connection with her family, the end of her father's pride and hope; Ricardo destroyed all the tapes he had of his daughter singing. Some people said that he had pushed his daughter too hard, and that the girl had given up on her singing before she met the African. At one Sunday lunch our host began to play a tape of the girl singing. This was done (as Ana and I knew, having been told beforehand) not to wound Ricardo, but to honour him and his daughter, and to help him with his grief. Our host had recently found the unmarked tape in his house; it was something he had made himself and forgotten about. And now we all listened to the girl singing in Italian and then in German, in the middle of the hot day, the light very bright outside. I found it moving (though I knew nothing about singing) that this kind of talent and ambition had come to someone living here. And Ricardo didn't make a scene. He looked down at the ground, crying, smiling with old pride, while his daughter sang on the tape with the voice and hopes of many years before.

The Noronhas were our blue-bloods, pure Portuguese. He was small and thin, and said to be a man of birth, but I don't know how true that was. She was deformed or disabled in some way – I never heard how, and never wanted to ask – and when she came among us she came in a wheelchair, which her husband pushed. They came into our half-and-half world with the gentlest air of condescension. They knew the country, and they knew where they stood and where we stood. It was possible to feel that they were breaking the rules only because the lady was disabled and had to be humoured. But the fact was that they came among us because of Mrs Noronha's special gifts. She was a 'mystic'. Her husband, the man of birth, was proud of this side of his wife. When they made their entry at an estate-house Sunday lunch he pushed her big wheelchair with a noticeable arrogance in his thin, peevish face. No one, not even Ana, ever told me directly that Mrs Noronha had this mystic gift. The gift was simply allowed to make itself felt, and it did so in such quiet ways that for the first few times I noticed nothing. To spot the gift at work, you had to know about it. Someone might say, for instance, 'I want to go to Lisbon next March.' Mrs Noronha, hunched up in her chair, would say softly, to no one in particular, 'It's not a good time. September would be better.' She would say no more, offer no explanation; and we wouldn't hear any more about a trip to Lisbon in March. And if – just for the sake of the illustration – if I, ignorant at that time of the lady's gifts, had said, 'But March in Lisbon would be lovely,' Mr Noronha would say, with distaste for the contradiction showing in his watery eyes, 'There are reasons why it's not a good time,' and his wife would look away, with no expression on her pale face. I felt that her mysticism, together with her disablement and her husband's birth, made her a tyrant. She could say anything; she could be as harsh and disdainful as she pleased; and for three or four or five good reasons no one could question her. I could see that from time to time she had spasms of pain, yet I couldn't help feeling that as soon as she and her husband got back home she might get out of her chair and be perfectly all right. She gave full mystical consultations. They were exclusive and not cheap; and these visitations among the half-and-half estate people, who were susceptible in more than one way, helped beat up custom.

Ana and I would also have had our characters. And, since no one can really see himself, I am sure that we would have been surprised and perhaps even wounded – just as the Correias and Ricardo and the Noronhas would have been surprised and wounded – by what the others saw.

This style of estate life would have begun in the 1920s, after the wartime boom. It would have become well established during the Second World War. So it was comparatively new; it could have been contained within the lifetime or even adulthood of a man. It didn't have much longer to go now; and I wonder whether in our circle we hadn't all (and not only the theatrical Correias) been granted some unsettling intimation, which we might have brushed aside, that our bluff in Africa would one day be called. Though I don't think anyone could have guessed that the world of concrete was going to be so completely overwhelmed by the frail old world of straw.

Sometimes we went for Sunday lunch to the rough weekend restaurant on the coast. It offered fresh seafood simply done, and it began to do well. It became less rough. When we went one Sunday we found the floor being tiled, in a pretty blue and yellow arabesque pattern that made us exclaim. The tiler was a big light-eyed mulatto man. For some reason – perhaps for not finishing the job on time – he was being abused and shouted at by the Portuguese owner. With us, and his other customers, the owner was as civil as always; but then, switching character and mood, he went back to abusing the tiler. At every shout the big light-eyed man lowered his head, as though he had received a blow. He was sweating; it seemed to be with more than heat. He went on with his delicate work, laying out the thin, fast-drying mortar, and then pressing and lightly tapping each pretty Portuguese tile into place. The sweat rolled down his pale-brown forehead and from time to time he shook it like tears from his eyes. He was in shorts; they were tight over his muscular thighs as he squatted. Little springs and twists of coarse hair were on his thighs and on his face, where close shaving had pock-marked the skin. He never replied to the shouts of the owner, whom he could so easily have knocked down. He just kept on working.

Ana and I talked afterwards about what we had seen. Ana said, 'The tiler is illegitimate. His mother would be African.

His father was almost certainly a big Portuguese landowner. The restaurant man would know that. The rich Portuguese put their illegitimate mulatto children to learning certain trades. Electrician, mechanic, metal-worker, carpenter, tiler. Though most of the tilers here come from the north of Portugal.'

I said nothing more to Ana. But whenever I remembered the big sweating man with the abused light eyes, carrying the shame of his birth on his face like a brand, I would think, 'Who will rescue that man? Who will avenge him?'

In time the emotion became mixed with other things. But the picture stayed. It was my own intimation of what was to come. And when, in my third year, the news began to leak into our controlled newspapers of big happenings on the other side of the continent, I was half ready for it.

The news was too big to suppress. The authorities might have wanted in the beginning to keep it quiet; but then they went the other way, and began to play up the horror. There had been an uprising in one region, and a mass killing of Portuguese in the countryside. Two hundred, three hundred, perhaps even four hundred, had died, and they had been done to death with machetes. I imagined a landscape like ours (though I knew this to be wrong), and Africans like ours, their huts and villages and cassava-and-corn plantings in the spaces between the big estates: the repeating neat acres of cashew and sisal, the great treeless cattle ranches looking like just-cleared wilderness, with the black trunks of big trees that had been felled or burnt to deny shelter to the poisonous flies that preyed on cattle. Order and logic; the land being made softer; but the picture I had had on my first day, of small-boned people always walking beside the road, had seemed dreamlike and threatening, telling me that the place I had come to was very far away. Now it seemed prophetic.

But the Africans around us seemed not to have heard anything. There was no change in their manner. Not that day or the next, not the next week or the next month. Correia, the man with the bank accounts, said that the ordinariness was ominous; some terrible *jacquerie* was preparing here as well. But the ordinariness stayed with us for the rest of the year, and seemed likely to endure. And all the precautions we had been taking – having guns and clubs to hand in the bedroom: futile if there had been anything like a general insurrection, or even a revolt in the quarters – began to seem excessive.

That was when I learned to use a gun. Word came to us and our neighbours, discreetly, that we could get instruction at the police shooting range in the town. The little garrison didn't have that facility, so unready was it for a war. Our neighbours were eager, but I didn't particularly want to go to the police range. I had never wanted to handle guns. There hadn't been anything like a cadet corps at the mission school; and my worry – greater than my worry about Africans – was that I was going to make a fool of myself before important people. But then, to my great surprise, I was entranced the first time I looked down a gun-sight with a finger on the trigger. It seemed to me the most private, the most intense moment of conversation with oneself, so to speak, with that split-second of right decision coming and going all the time, almost answering the movements of one's mind. It wasn't at all what I was expecting. I feel that the religious excitement that is supposed to come to people who meditate on the flame of a single candle in an otherwise dark room was no greater than the pleasure I felt when I looked down a gun-sight and became very close to my own mind and consciousness. In a second the scale of things could alter and I could be lost in something like a private universe. It was strange, being on the shooting range in Africa and thinking in a new way of my father and his brahmin ancestors, starveling servants of the great temple. I bought a gun. I set up targets in the grounds of Ana's grandfather's house and practised whenever I could. Our neighbours began to look at me with a new regard.

The government took its time, but then things began to move. The garrison was increased. There were new barracks, three storeys high, in bright white concrete. The cantonment or military area spread, plain concrete on bare sand. A board with various military emblems said that we had become the headquarters of a new military command. The life of the town altered.

* * *

THE GOVERNMENT was authoritarian. But most of the time we didn't think of it like that. We felt the government to be far away, something in the capital, something in Lisbon. It sat lightly on us here. I worried about it only at sisal-cutting time, when we made our requisitions from the prisons, and they, for a consideration, sent convicts (properly guarded) to cut sisal. Cutting sisal was dangerous work. Village Africans didn't want to do it. Sisal is like a bigger aloe or pineapple plant, or like a giant spiky green rose, four or five feet high, with thick pulpy blades instead of petals. The blades have cutting serrated edges, frightful to run your hand down the wrong way, and are very thick at the base. They are awkward and dangerous to handle and hard to hack away. The long black point at the end of a sisal blade is needle-sharp and poisonous. Rats are plentiful in a sisal plantation; they like the shade and feed on sisal pulp; and venomous snakes come to feed on the rats, swallowing them whole, and very slowly. It is frightening to see half a rat, head or tail, sticking out of a snake's distended mouth and still apparently living. A sisal plantation is a terrible place, and it was a rule (or just our practice) that a medical nurse should be standing by with medicines and snake-bite serum when sisal was being cut. Such dangerous work; and only five per cent of sisal pulp became sisal fibre; and that fibre was cheap and was used in ordinary things like rope and baskets and sandal soles. Without the convicts it would have been hard to harvest our sisal. Even at that time synthetic fibre was beginning to replace it. I didn't mind at all.

There had been no challenge to our authoritarian but easy-going government for many years, and it had grown strangely lazy. In his great security the ruler had grown to feel that the details of governing were a burden, or so it appeared; and he had farmed out or leased out important governmental activities to eager, energetic, and loyal people. Those people became very rich; and the richer they became the more loyal they were, and the better they did the jobs that had been farmed out to them. So there was a kind of rough logic and effectiveness in this principle of government.

Some such principle was at work now in the growth of the garrison and the development of our town. The peace was continuing. People no longer lived with the idea of danger. Yet year by year the war money came. It touched us all. We felt rewarded and virtuous. Everybody counted his gain many times. And then it came out that the new money had been touching our friend Correia more than anybody else in our group, sly Correia who for years had tried to frighten us with his vision of disaster, and had many bank accounts abroad. Correia had been brought into contact with some great man in the capital, and (while still running his estate) he had become the agent in our town or province, or perhaps even the country, for a number of foreign manufacturers of unlikely-sounding technical things. In the beginning Correia liked to boast of his closeness to the great man, who was a proper Portuguese. The great man clearly had a lot to do with Correia's agencies, and we talked among ourselves in a mocking, jealous way about the extraordinary relationship. Had Correia sought out the great man? Or had the great man, for some special reason, and through some intermediary (perhaps a merchant in the capital) chosen Correia? It didn't matter, though, how it had come about. Correia had scored. He was way above us.

He talked of trips to the capital (by air, and not by the dingy old coasting ships most of us still used); he talked of lunches and dinners with the great man, and once even of a dinner at the great man's house. But then after a while Correia talked less of the great man. He began to pretend, when he was with us, that his business ideas were his own; and we had to pretend with him. Though when he recited the foreign companies he was involved with, and the technical-sounding things he was importing, things that the army or the town might some day need, I found myself amazed at how little I knew of the modern world. And amazed at the same time at the ease with which Correia (who really knew only about estate work) was picking his way through it.

He became our big shot. When he found that the jealousy had subsided, and no one among us, his friends and neighbours, was quibbling about his new position, he became oddly modest. He said to me one Sunday, 'You could do what I do, Willie. It's just a matter of courage. Let me tell you. You've spent time in England. You know the Boots shops. Over here we need the things they make, the medicines and other things. They have no agent. You could be the agent. So you write to them. You provide the references they will ask for, and you're in business. They'll be delighted.' I said, 'But what am I going to do with the goods they send me? How am I going to start selling it? Where am I going to put it?' He said, 'That's the trouble. To do business you have to be in business. You have to start thinking in a different way. You can't write to people like Boots and think they'll want to do business with you just for a year and a day.' And I thought, from the way he talked, that he and his principal had gone quite seriously into the Boots business, and nothing had come of it.

He said one Sunday that he had begun to think of representing a certain famous manufacturer of helicopters. That took our breath away, because we knew now that he wasn't joking, and it gave us some idea how big he had become. He seemed to know a lot about helicopters. He said the idea had come to him all at once – he made it sound like a saint's illumination – when he was driving along the road to the coast. He talked about helicopters for many weeks. And then we read in the controlled press – in an item we might have paid no attention to if we didn't know Correia – that a number of helicopters were being acquired, but of a different make from the one Correia had talked about. We heard no more from him about helicopters.

So Correia became rich – the helicopter business was only a stumble – and he and his wife spoke in their old simple-minded way about their money. Yet they still had that idea of the disaster to come. Their good fortune had made them more worried than ever, and they said they had decided not to spend their money in the colony. The only thing they did here was to buy a beach house, not far from the restaurant we used to go to, in a holiday area that was now opening up fast. They did that as an 'investment'. It was one of their new words. They formed a company called Jacar Investments; and they passed around to us, as to country cousins they had left behind, cards printed with the stylish name, which combined elements of their first names, Jacinto and Carla. They travelled a lot because of their new business, but now they didn't only open bank accounts. They began to think of getting 'papers' for various places – making us feel even more left behind – and on their travels they set matters in train: papers for Australia, papers for Canada, papers for the United States, papers for Argentina and Brazil. They even talked – or Carla talked one Sunday – of going to live in France. They had just been there, and they brought a bottle of a famous French wine for the Sunday lunch. There was a half-glass for everybody, and everybody sipped and said what nice wine it was, though it was actually too acid. Carla said, 'The

French know how to live. A flat on the Left Bank, and a little house in Provence – that would be very nice. I've been telling Jacinto.' And we who were not going to France sipped the acid wine like poison.

After some years of this – when it seemed that to the success of the Correias there could be no end, as long as the army was there, and the town was growing, and the great man was in his place in the capital – after some years there was a crisis. We knew it by the Correias' behaviour. They drove an hour and a half every morning to the mission church and heard mass. Three hours' driving, and an hour's mass, every day, and heaven knows how many prayers or novenas or whatever at home: it wasn't the kind of behaviour anyone could keep secret. Jacinto Correia grew pale and thin. Then we read in the controlled newspapers that irregularities had been uncovered on the procurement side. For some weeks the newspapers allowed the scandal to spark away, and then the great pure Portuguese man with whom Jacinto Correia was connected made a statement in the local executive council. In everything that concerned the public weal, the great man said, the government had to be ever vigilant, and he intended, without fear or favour, to get to the bottom of what had happened on the procurement side. The guilty would be brought to book; no one in the colony should doubt that.

It was the other side of the easy-going authoritarian state, and we knew that the Correias were in deep trouble, that neither bank accounts in great cities, nor papers for great countries, could rescue them. Darkness here was darkness.

Poor Carla said, 'I never wanted this life. The nuns will tell you. I wanted to be a nun.'

And we knew then – it was something we had talked about for years among ourselves – why Correia had been chosen by the great man. It was for just such a moment, when the great man might have to throw someone into the darkness. To destroy a Portuguese like himself would have been to break caste, according to the code of the colony, and to become disreputable. There was no trouble at all in throwing a man of the second rank into the darkness, someone from the half-and-half world, educated and respectable and striving, unusually knowledgeable about money, and ready for many reasons to do whatever he might be required to do.

For three or four months the Correias lived with this torment. They dreamed all the time of simpler days, before the agencies, and all the time they rebuked themselves. Our hearts went out to them; but their wretchedness also made them tedious. Jacinto became like an invalid, living with his disease as with an enemy and thinking of little else. And then, abruptly, the crisis was over. Jacinto's great man in the capital had found some way of putting down the rival who had started all the mischief. The newspapers then stopped writing their poisonous paragraphs, and the procurement scandal (which had existed only in the newspapers) simply ceased to be.

But it wasn't the end of Jacinto's anxiety. He had been given an idea of the uncertain ways of power. He knew now that he might not always have the protection of a great man, and then, for any number of reasons, someone might wish to reopen the case against him. So he suffered. And in one way that was strange, since for years we had heard Jacinto talk (and sometimes with zest) of a calamity to come, something that would sweep away the life of the colony, sweep away all his world. A man who lived easily with that idea (and liked to frighten people with it) shouldn't have worried for a moment about the schemings of a few vengeful people in the capital – all doomed, anyway. But Jacinto's big event, which was going to take away everybody and everything, was a philosophical sham. As soon as you looked at it you saw that it was very vague. It really was a moral idea and a way of self-absolution, a way of living in the colony and at the same time standing outside it. It was an abstraction. The disgrace he was worried about was not abstract. It was very real, easy to work out in many of its details; and it was personal. It was going to fall on him alone and leave the rest of the whole sweet world untouched.

One Sunday, when it was our turn to give the lunch, we went to the beach restaurant with the yellow and blue tiled floor. It was Correia's idea afterwards that we should all go to see his beach house, the investment. Ana and I and many of the others had never seen it, and he said he hadn't been there for two years. We drove from the restaurant back to the narrow asphalt coast road, a black crust on the sand, and after a while we turned off into a firm sandy road that led between brilliant green sand shrubs and tropical almond trees back to the sea. We saw an African hut, its smooth grass roof shining and almost auburn in the light. We stopped. Correia called out, 'Auntie! Auntie!' An old black woman in an African cloth came out from behind the straight reed fence. Correia said to us, 'Her son is half-Portuguese. He is the caretaker.' He was loud and friendly with the African woman, overdoing it a little, perhaps to show off to us, acting out the twin roles of the man who got on with Africans and the employer who treated his people well. The woman was worried. She was resisting Correia's role-playing. Correia asked for Sebastião. Sebastião wasn't at home. And we followed Correia, who was making a lot of noise, to the house on the beach.

We found a half-ruin. Windows had been broken; in the moist salt air nails had rusted everywhere, and the rust had run, staining faded paint and bleached wood. The french doors on the ground floor had been taken off their hinges. Half in and half out of what should have been the sitting room there was a high-sided fishing boat propped up on timbers as in a dry dock.

The old African woman stood some distance behind Correia. He said nothing. He just looked. His face creased and went strange. He was beyond anger, and far away from the scene about him. He was helpless, drowning in pain. I thought, 'He's mad. I wonder why I never saw it before.' And it was as if Carla, the convent girl, was used to living with what I had just seen. She went to him and, as though we were not there, talked to him as to a child, using language I had never heard her use. She said, 'We'll burn the fucking place down. I'll go and get the kerosene right now and we'll come back and burn the whole damned thing, with the fucking boat.' He said nothing, and allowed her to lead him by the arm back to the car, past Auntie's hut.

When we next saw them, some weeks later, he looked drained. His thin cheeks were soft and slack. Carla said, 'We're going to Europe for a while.'

Mrs Noronha, hunched up in her chair, said in her soft voice, 'A bad time.' Carla said, 'We want to go and see the children.' The Correias' two children, who were in their teens, had been sent a year or so before to boarding schools in Portugal. Mrs Noronha said, 'A better time for them.' And then, without any change of tone, 'What's the matter with the boy? Why is he so ill?' Carla became agitated. She said, 'I didn't know he was ill. He hasn't written that.'

Mrs Noronha paid no attention. She said, 'I made a journey once at a bad time. It was not long after the war. And it was long before I took to this chair. Before I took the throne, you might say. We went to South Africa, to Durban. A pretty town, but it was a bad time. About a week after we got there the natives began to riot. Shop-burning, looting. The riots were against the Indians, but I got caught up in the trouble one day. I didn't know what to do. I didn't know the streets. In the distance I saw a white lady with fair hair and a long dress. She beckoned to me and I went to her. She led me without a word through various side streets to a big house, and there I stayed until the streets were quiet. I told my friends about the incident that evening. They said, "What was this lady like?" I told them. They said, "Describe the house." I described the house. And somebody said, "But that house was pulled down twenty years ago. The lady you met lived there, and the house was pulled down after she died."' And having told her story, which was really about her own powers, Mrs Noronha turned her head to one side, against her shoulder, like a bird settling down to sleep. And, as often with her when she was soothsaying or story-telling, we couldn't tell at the end how we had got to where we had got. Everybody just had to look solemn and stay quiet for a while.

Bad time or not, the Correias went off to Europe, to see
their children and then to do other things. They stayed away
for many months.

* * *

I GOT TO KNOW their estate manager. I saw a lot of him in
the town. He was a small and wiry mixed-race man in his
forties with an educated way of speaking. Sometimes he could
overdo it. He would say, for instance, about a Portuguese or
Indian shopkeeper with whom he had been having trouble,
'He isn't, by the remotest stretch of the imagination, what
you would call a gentleman.' But his speech limbered up when
he saw more of me. He became full of mischief, and at the
same time quite trusting, and I felt I was being drawn into a
series of little conspiracies against the Correias. We tried the
new cafés (they opened up and closed down all the time).
We got to know the bars. I got to know the new flavour of
the military town, and I liked it. I liked being with the
Portuguese soldiers. There was sometimes an officer with a
long memory muttering about Goa and the Indians. But the
Indian takeover of Goa had happened seven or eight years
before. Few of the young conscripts knew about it, and the
soldiers were generally very friendly. There was as yet no
war in the bush. There had been stories about guerrilla
training camps in the desert in Algeria and later in Jordan;
but these stories had turned out to be fanciful: a few students
from Lisbon and Coimbra playing at being guerrillas in the
vacations. In our military town there was still peace and a
great deal of civility. It was like being in Europe, and on

holiday. It was for me like being in London again, but with money now. My excursions to the town took longer and longer.

Álvaro, the Correias' manager, said to me one day, 'Would you like to see what *they* do?' We were in a café in the capital, having a coffee before driving home, and he lifted his chin at a group of brightly dressed African women, brilliant in the mid-afternoon light, who were passing in front of the café window. Normally the afternoon view was of torpid begging children, very dusty, who leaned on walls or shop windows or posts, opened and closed their mouths in slow motion all the time, and seemed not to see anything. Even when you gave them money they seemed not to know; and they never went away, however much you gave them; you had to learn to ignore them. The women were not like that. They were quite regal. I supposed they were camp-followers, and I said to Álvaro that I would like to see what they did. He said, 'I'll come for you tomorrow evening. It's much better in the evenings, and it's much better at the weekends. You'll have to find some way of making your excuses to Madame Ana.'

Álvaro made it sound easy, but I found it hard. In ten years I hadn't lied to Ana; there hadn't been the occasion. In the beginning, in London, when I couldn't see my way ahead, I had fabricated things, mainly about my family background. I don't know how much of that Ana believed, or whether it meant much to her. In Africa I had after a while let those London lies drop; in our half-and-half group they seemed to have no point. Over the years Ana had picked up the truth about me. It wasn't too different from what she had always believed; and she had never made me feel small by reminding me of the stories I had told her. In Africa we were very close, and that closeness seemed natural. She had given me my African life; she was my protector; I had no other anchor. So I found it hard to make my excuses to her. It spoilt the next day. I began to work out a story. It felt like a lie. I tried to straighten it out, and it became too involved. I thought, 'I am going to sound like someone from the quarters.' And then I thought, 'I am going back to my London ways.' When the time came Ana hardly listened to what I had to say. She said, 'I hope Carla is going to have an estate to come back to.' It was as easy as that. But I knew I had broken something, put an end to something, for almost no reason.

Álvaro was dead on time; he might have been waiting in the dark just outside the estate compound. I thought that we would be going to the town, but Álvaro didn't make for the main road. Instead, we drove slowly about the backways, all ordinary to me now, even at night. I thought that Álvaro was killing time. We drove, now past cotton fields, now through open bush, now past dark plantations of cashew trees. Every few miles we came to a village, and then we drove very slowly. Sometimes in a village there was a kind of night market, with petty stalls in low open huts, lit by a hurricane lantern, selling matches and loose cigarettes and small tins of various things, and with a few improvident people, men or women or children, finding themselves penniless that day and sitting at the roadside with candles in paper bags beside very small heaps of their own food, sticks of dried cassava, or peppers, or vegetables. Like people playing at housekeeping, and playing at buying and selling, I had always thought.

Álvaro said, 'Pretty, eh?' I knew some of these villages
very well. I had seen these night markets scores of times. It
wasn't what I had come out to see with Álvaro. He said, 'You
wanted to see what the Africans did at night. I'm showing
you. You've been here ten years. I don't know how much you
know. In a couple of hours these roads we've been driving
along will be crawling with people looking for adventure.
There will be twenty or thirty parties tonight all around you.
Did you know that? And they aren't going there just to
dance, I can tell you.'

The headlights of the Land-Rover picked out, just in time,
a little girl in a shoulder-strap dress ahead of us. She stood
at the side of the road and, shiny-faced in the lights, watched
us pass. Álvaro said, 'How old do you think that girl is?' I
really hadn't thought; the girl was like so many others;
I wouldn't have recognised her again. Álvaro said, 'I will
tell you. That girl is about eleven. She's had her first period,
and that means that she's ready for sex. The Africans are
very sensible about these things. No foreign nonsense about
under-age sex. That girl who looks like nothing to you is
screwing every night with some man. Am I telling you
things you know?' I said, 'You are telling me things I don't
know.' He said, 'It's what we think about you, you know.
I hope you don't mind.' And really in ten years I had never
looked in that way at the villages and the Africans walking
beside the road. I suppose it was a lack of curiosity, and
I suppose it was a remnant of caste feeling. But then, too, I
wasn't of the country, hadn't been trained in its sexual ways
(though I had observed them), and had never before had
someone like Álvaro as a guide.

In the very beginning, when I hadn't even known about the pleasures of living in the wilderness, I had thought that the mixed-race overseers couldn't have had much of a life, living so close to Africans, surrendering so much of themselves. Now I saw that for some it would have been a life of constant excitement. Álvaro lived in a dingy four-roomed concrete house. It stood by itself on an exposed, treeless patch on Correia's estate. It looked a comfortless place to call home, but Álvaro lived happily there with his African wife and African family, and with any number of mistresses or concubines or pick-ups within reach in the surrounding villages. In no other part of the world would Álvaro have found a life like that. I had thought at the beginning of the evening that he was killing time, driving about the backways. He wasn't. He was trying to show where hidden treasure lay. He said, 'Take that little girl we just passed. If you stopped to ask her the way she would stick up her little breasts at you, and she would know what she was doing.' And I began to understand that Álvaro was already wound up, thinking of that little girl or some other girl sticking up her little breasts at him.

At last we made for the main road. It was badly potholed after the rains. We couldn't see too far ahead, and we had to drive slowly. Every now and then we came to a rock cone. For a while before and after it seemed to hang over us in the darkness, marking off another stage to the town. The town was alive but not raucous. The street lights were scattered and not too bright. Here and there in the central area a fluorescent tube turned a shop window into a box of light, not to advertise the shoddy goods in the higgledy-piggledy display, but to keep away thieves. The weak blue light, teasing the eye, didn't travel far in the darkness of the street, where during the day loaders, or men who could wait all morning or afternoon for a loading job, sat with their legs wide apart on the steps of shops, and where now another kind of lounger waited for whatever might come his way from the new traffic of the garrison town. Álvaro said, 'It's better to steer clear of those fellows. You have no control over them.'

And just as at the start of the evening he had driven around the backways of the estates so now he drove around the quieter streets of the town, sometimes getting out of the Land-Rover to talk in a confidential voice to people he saw. He told me he was looking for a good dancing place; they changed all the time, he said. It was better than going to a bar. They could be brutal places, bars. In a bar you didn't deal with the girl alone; you also dealt with her protector, who might be one of the loungers in the street. And in a bar there were no facilities. When you found a girl you had to go out with her to some dark passage between houses in the town or to some house in the African city, the straw city, as it was called, at the edge of the town, and all that time you would be at the mercy of the protector. It was all right for a soldier, but it was bad for an estate manager. If there was an unpleasantness with the protector, word would get back in no time to the estate, and there could be trouble with the workers.

At last we came to the place Álvaro had been looking for. I imagined it was a place with facilities. He said, 'It's as our elders say. If you ask often enough, you can get to Rome.' We were at the edge of the town, where the asphalt roads ended and dirt began, much cut up by the rains. It was dark, with only a few scattered lights, and so quiet that the slamming of the Land-Rover doors was like a disturbance.

We had stopped in front of a big warehouse-like building. High at one corner was a metal-shaded bulb misty and twinkling with flying ants (it was the season). Other cars were parked in the space in front; and we saw now that there were watchmen of a sort (or just watchers) sitting on a half-wall on one side of the warehouse lot, where the land fell away. One of these watchers spoke directions to us, and we went down a concrete passage between the warehouse and the half-wall to another warehouse-like building. We heard music inside. A small door opened, a man with a truncheon let us in, and we both gave him money. The entrance passage was narrow and dark and it made a hairpin bend before it took us to the main room. Blue light bulbs lit up a small dancing area. Two couples were dancing – Portuguese men, African women – and they were reflected, dimly, in the dark mirror or mirror-tiles that covered the wall at the end of the dancing area. The room was full of tables with low shaded lights, but it wasn't easy to see how many of them were occupied. We didn't move in far. We sat at a table on the edge of the dancing area. Across the way were the girls, like the courtesans of the previous afternoon who had been pleased to walk down the street in their pretty clothes, turning heads. When I got used to the light I saw that many of the girls on the other side of the dancing area were not village girls from the interior, but were what we called Mohammedans, people of the coast, of remote Arab ancestry. Two African waiters and a thin Portuguese man in a sports shirt – the owner, I suppose – moved between the tables. When the Portuguese man came close to us I saw that he was not young, had very quiet eyes, and seemed strangely detached from everything.

I wish I had his detachment. But I was not trained for this kind of life, and I was full of shame. The girls were all African. It had to be like that, I suppose; but I wondered whether the two African waiters didn't suffer a little. And the girls were so young, so foolish, with so little idea, as I thought, of the way they were abusing their own bodies and darkening their lives. I thought with old unhappiness of things at home. I thought of my mother and I thought of my poor father who had hardly known what sex was. I thought of you, too, Sarojini. I imagined that the girls might be you, and my heart shrank.

Álvaro himself was subdued. He had been subdued as soon as he had entered the dark warehouse. He was excited by village sex, with every month a fresh crop of innocent girls who had had their first period and were ready to stick up their little breasts at him. What was around us in this half-converted warehouse was different. I don't suppose a place like this, with facilities, would have existed before the army came. It would have been new to Álvaro. And I suppose that though he was casting himself as my guide, he really was a learner, a little nervous, and he needed my support.

We drank beer. The feeling of shame went. I looked at the dancers in the blue light, and their dim reflections in the mysterious space of the wall-high dark mirror. I had never seen Africans dance. With the kind of estate life I had been living there hadn't been the occasion. Immediately these girls began to dance they were touched by a kind of grace. The gestures were not extravagant; they could be very small. When a girl danced she incorporated everything into her dance – her conversation with her partner, a word spoken over her shoulder to a friend, a laugh. This was more than pleasure; it was as though some deeper spirit was coming out in the dance. This spirit was locked up in every girl, whatever her appearance; and it was possible to feel that it was part of something much larger. Of course, with my background, I had thought a lot about Africans in a political way. In the warehouse I began to have an idea that there was something in the African heart that was shut away from the rest of us, and beyond politics.

Álvaro, with a little grimace of self-mockery which didn't fool me, began to dance with one of the girls. At first he clowned on the floor, looking at himself in the mirror. But very soon he became dead serious, and when he came back to our table he was a changed man. His eyes were hollow with longing. He frowned at his beer glass. Then he said, with an affectation of anger, as though everybody in that room was holding him back, 'I don't know what thoughts you have on the subject, Willie. But now that we are in this bloody place I'm going to have a damned little something.' And, frowning hard, like a man in a rage, he went with his dancing partner to the door in the dark far part of the room.

I might have just stayed and sipped beer and waited for Álvaro. But the quiet-eyed Portuguese man knew his business, and three or four or five minutes later, at a signal from him, one of the girls came and sat at the table. Below her fussy clothes she was quite small. Below the make-up, the rouge on the high cheekbones, the white-blue paint on the eyelids, she was very young. I looked at her 'Arab' face and, only a half or a quarter trying to stimulate myself, wondered what about her would have aroused Álvaro. When she got up and invited me to follow her, I did. We went to the little door in the dark corner. There were a number of cubicles off a concrete passage. The partitions did not go all the way to the ceiling, and all the cubicles were served by two naked bulbs high on the back wall. I supposed that if I listened hard enough I might have heard Álvaro. The warehouse had been converted and given its facilities in the cheapest way. The place could have closed down at any time, and the owner would not have lost.

Without her stiff clothes the girl was really very small. But she was firm and hard; she would have done much physical work as a child. Ana was not like that; Ana was bony and frail. I felt the girl's breasts; they were small and only slightly less hard than the rest of her. Álvaro would have liked those breasts; it was possible to imagine the stiff young nipples sticking up below a cheap village cotton dress. But the nipples of this little girl were broad and spongy at the tip: she had already had a child or children. I couldn't feel any longing for her. Even if I did, all the old ghosts were already with me, the ghosts of home, the ghosts of London eleven or twelve years before, the awful prostitute in Soho, the big hips of June on the mattress on the floor in the slum house in Notting Hill, all the shame and incompetence. I didn't think that anything was going to happen to me with the poor little girl below me on the cheap, army-reject mattress.

So far the girl's eyes had been blank. But then, just at the moment when I was about to fail, an extraordinary look of command and aggression and need filled those eyes, her body became all tension, and I was squeezed by her strong hands and legs. In a split-second – like the split-second of decision when I looked down a gun-sight – I thought, 'This is what Álvaro lives for,' and I revived.

Álvaro and I were both subdued afterwards. Álvaro became himself again, bouncy and knowing, only when we were near the estate house. The pressure lamp had been left on for me above the semi-circular entrance steps. Ana was asleep in her grandfather's big carved bed. Two hours or so before I had thought of her in an unfair and belittling way. I needed a shower before I could lie down beside her. The antiquated fittings in the bathroom – the Portguese-made geyser, the tricky shower-head, the minutely cracked wash-basin with decorated metal supports – still made me feel a stranger. They made me think of everyone who had slept in that big carved bed before me: Ana's grandfather, turning away from the African woman who had borne his children; Ana's mother, betrayed by her husband and then by her lover; and Ana's father, who had betrayed everybody. I didn't feel that evening that I had betrayed Ana in any important or final way. I could say with truth that what had happened had been empty, that I had felt no longing and no true satisfaction. But locked away in my mind was that split-second when the girl had looked at me with command and I had felt the tension and strength in her small body. I could think of no reason why I had done what I had done. But I began to think, almost in another part of my mind, that there must have been some reason.

And just as, after a long or strenuous or dangerous drive,

the road continues to speed by in the mind of the driver as he settles down to sleep, so that split-second with the girl flashed again and again before me as I lay beside Ana. And it drew me back, within a week, to the converted warehouse on the edge of the town, to the blue bulbs and the dance floor and the little cubicles. This time I made no excuses to Ana.

I began to live with a new idea of sex, a new idea of my capacity. It was like being given a new idea of myself. We are all born with sexual impulses, but we are not all born with sexual skill, and there are no schools where we can be trained. People like me have to fumble and stumble on as best they can, and wait for accidents to take them to something like knowledge. I was thirty-three. All I had known so far – leaving out London, which really didn't count – was what I had had with Ana. Just after we had come to Africa we had been passionate. Or I had been passionate. There would have been some genuine excitement there, some moments of sexual discovery. But a fair part of that passion of ten years before would have come not out of sensuality or true desire but out of my own nervousness and fear, like a child's fear, at being in Africa, at having thrown myself into a void. There had been nothing like that passion between us since then. Ana, even at that time of passion, had been half timorous; and when I had been admitted into more of her family history I understood her timorousness. So in a way we were matched. We each found comfort in the other; and we had become very close, not looking beyond the other for satisfaction, not knowing, in fact, that another kind of satisfaction was possible. And if Álvaro hadn't come along I would have continued in that way, in matters of sex and sensuality not much above my poor deprived father.

The warehouse closed down after a while; then something else came up; and something else after that. The concrete town was very small; the merchants and civil servants and others who lived there didn't want these places of pleasure too near their houses and their families. So the blue bulbs and the dark wall-high mirror shifted about from one makeshift home to another. It was worth no one's while to build something more permanent, since the army, on which the trade depended, could at any time move away.

One evening I saw, among the rouged and dressed-up girls, Júlio the carpenter's daughter – the little maid who on my first morning had laid aside her broom and sat in a worn upholstered chair and tried to have an educated conversation with me. She had told me later that her family ate the same food every day; and that when her father became too drunken or violent she tried to lull herself to sleep by walking up and down in the little room they had. The story later was that this girl had begun to drink, like her father, and was often out of the quarters. I suppose that just as Álvaro had been my guide some friend had guided her here.

I decided on the spur of the moment not to see her; and she seemed to have decided on the same thing. So that when we crossed we crossed as strangers. I told no one about her; and she, when we next met in the estate house, said nothing at all and made not even a small gesture of new recognition. She didn't widen her eyes or lift her brow or set her mouth. When I thought about it later I felt that that was when I betrayed Ana, sullied her, as it were, in her own house.

* * *

THE CORREIAS HAD been away for a year. And then we heard, each house in a roundabout way, and not all at the same time, that Jacinto had died. He had died in his sleep in a hotel in London. Álvaro was in a state. He didn't know what his future was. He had always dealt with Jacinto; and he had a feeling that Carla didn't care for him.

About a month later Carla reappeared among us, visiting the houses she knew, harvesting sympathy. Again and again she told of the suddenness of the death, of the shopping that had just been done in the big stores, the opened parcels left untidily that night about what was to be poor Jacinto's deathbed. She had thought of bringing back the body to the colony; but she had a 'bad feeling' (given her by Mrs Noronha) about the little cemetery in the town. So she had taken the body to Portugal, to the country town where Jacinto's full Portuguese grandfather was buried. All of this had kept her too busy for grief. That came to her afterwards. It came to her especially when she saw some beggars in Lisbon. She said, 'I thought, "These people have nothing to live for, and yet they're living. Jacinto had so much to live for, and yet he's dead."' The unfairness was too much for her to bear. She had burst out crying in the public street, and the beggars who had approached her had become agitated; some of them even begged her pardon. (Ana told me later, 'I always used to think that Jacinto believed that if you became rich enough you weren't going to die. Or he wasn't going to die, if he became rich enough. But I used to think of that as a joke. I didn't know it was true.')

Jacinto had always been particular about the distinction that money brought to people, Carla said; that was why he had worked so hard. He had told his children, who were studying in Lisbon, that they were on no account to use public transport in Lisbon. They were always to use taxis. People must never think of them as colonial nobodies. He had repeated that to them only a few days before he had died. And telling this story about Jacinto's concern for his children, and other related stories about the goodness of the family man, Carla wept and wept from estate house to estate house.

With Álvaro she was brutal. Three weeks after she came back she sacked him, giving him and his African family a month to clear out of their concrete house; and, to make it harder for him to find work, she did what she could to blacken his character with estate people. He was a man of loose life, she said, with a string of African concubines he couldn't possibly keep on his manager's salary. Even when Jacinto was having his trouble with the people in the capital, he used to tell her that she had to watch Álvaro. The rogue had trembled when she called for the books. She didn't have Jacinto's mind, and she didn't know much about accounts, but it didn't take her long to see the kind of trickery Jacinto had told her to look out for. Bogus invoices (with Álvaro machinery had broken down all the time, even the reliable old German sisal-crusher, the simplest of machines, like a very big mangle); inflated real invoices; and, of course, bogus workers. And the longer the Correias had stayed away in Europe the more brazen Álvaro had become.

Carla was telling us what we all half knew. In his foolish, showing-off way Álvaro had liked to hint that he was milking the estate. He had done that with me and he would have done it with others. He thought it made him grand, almost like an estate-owner. Estate life was all that Álvaro knew; the estate house was his idea of style. His father, a mulatto, had started as a mechanic on the estate owned by his Portuguese father, and had ended there as a low-grade overseer living in one of a line of two-roomed concrete houses. Álvaro decided when he was quite young that he would rise in the world. He was good with machines; he learned about cattle and crops; he knew how to get on with Africans. He rose; he became flashy. As the Correias' estate manager, with a proper concrete house and a Land-Rover, he liked to make big gestures. When I got to know him (and before I knew his reputation) he used to give me presents; afterwards he would tell me that what he had given me was really plunder from the Correias.

Still, I felt sorry for Álvaro that he should be so exposed and pulled down in the estate houses where (leaving his African family at home) he wanted to be accepted. I wondered how that family were going to make out. They had got their marching orders and would soon have to leave their concrete house; it would be some time before they got accommodation like that again. Ana said, 'He might take the opportunity to forget about them.' I didn't want to think about that too much, but it was probably true. Álvaro had never spoken of his family to me, had never given his children names or characters. I had seen them only from the road: African-looking children, some like village children, staring from the small verandah of the concrete house or running out from the grass-roofed kitchen hut at the back. I suppose if a new job came up Álvaro wouldn't have minded moving on and starting afresh with a new woman and new outside women in a new place. He might have considered an outcome like that a blessing; it would have reconciled him to everything.

I hadn't seen him for some weeks. We had long ago stopped making excursions together to places like the warehouse. And when one day we met on the asphalt road to the town he was subdued; the humiliation of his sacking and the worry showed on his face. He was defiant, though. He said, 'I don't know who the hell these people think they are, Willie. It's all going up in smoke. They are going to Lisbon and Paris and London and talking about their children's education. They are living in a fool's paradise.' I thought he was copying the apocalyptic tone of his late master. But he had real news. He said, 'The guerrillas are in camps just over the border. The government there is on their side. They are real guerrillas now, and they aren't playing. When they decide to move I don't see what's going to stop them.'

For some weeks there had been fewer soldiers in the town, and there had been talk about army manoeuvres deep in the bush to the north and the west. There was little in the newspapers. It was only later, some time after Álvaro had given me the news, that announcements were made of the successful army 'sweep' to the north and west, right up to the border. The army began then to come back to the town;

and things were as before. The places of pleasure were busy again. But by this time I had lost touch with Álvaro.

I had found less and less pleasure in the places of pleasure. Some of this would have had to do with my worry about seeing Júlio's daughter again. But the main reason was that the act of sex there, which used to excite me with its directness and brutality, had grown mechanical. For the first year I used to keep a tally, in my head, of the times I had been; again and again I would do the sums, associating outside events, lunches, visits, with these darker, brighter moments in the warm cubicles, creating as it were a special calendar of that year for myself. Gradually, then, it happened that I went not out of need but in order to add to the tally. At an even later stage I went just to test my capacity. Sometimes on those occasions I had to drive myself; I wished then not to extend the moment but to finish as soon as possible. The girls were always willing, always ready to demonstrate the tricks of strength and suppleness that had sent me away the first time with new sensations, a new idea of myself, and tenderness for everyone and everything. Now the sensation was of exhaustion and waste, of my lower stomach scraped dry; I needed a day or two to recover. It was in this enervated mood that I began to make love to Ana again, hoping to recover the closeness that had once seemed so natural. It couldn't be. That old closeness was not based on love-making, and now, not even rebuking me for my long absence, she was as timorous as I remembered. I gave her little pleasure; I gave myself none at all. So I was more restless and dissatisfied than I had been before Álvaro said to me in the café in the town, 'Would you like to see what *they* do?' Before I had been introduced to a kind of sensual life I didn't know I was missing.

* * *

CARLA ANNOUNCED THAT she was going to move to Portugal for good as soon as she found a new manager. The news cast a gloom over us, people of Carla's estate-house group, and we tried over the next few weeks to get her to change her mind, not because we were thinking of her, but because – as often after a death – we were thinking of ourselves. We were jealous and worried. Carla's going away, the disappearance of the Correias, felt like the beginning of the breakdown of our special world. It touched new fears we didn't want to think about; it lessened our idea of the life we were leading. Even Ana, never envious of anyone, said with something like spite, 'Carla says she's leaving because she can't bear to be alone in the house, but I happen to know that she's only doing what Jacinto told her to do.'

Soon enough the new manager was found. He was the husband of a convent-school friend of Carla's; and the story, spread by Carla to win sympathy for the couple, was that life had not treated them well. They were not going to live in the manager's house; Álvaro and his family had left that (and the huts they had added on) in a great mess. They were going to live in the estate house. Ana said, 'Carla talks about charity to a friend who has fallen on hard times. But that friend is going to have to keep the house in good order. Carla came back from Europe to a house that had begun to fall apart. I feel it in my bones that Carla is going to sell in a couple of years, when the market rises.'

There was a special Sunday lunch at the house, to say goodbye to Carla, and to meet the new manager. Even if I didn't know about his circumstances I would have noticed him. There was about him a quality of suppressed violence; he was like a man holding himself in check. He was in his forties, of mixed ancestry, more Portuguese than African, broad but soft-looking. He was polite to everybody, even formal, anxious in one way to make a good impression, yet different in manner and style from everyone, a man apart. His eyes were distant; they seemed a little bit removed from what he was doing. The bumps on his top lip were pronounced; the lower lip was full and smooth, with a shine; it was the mouth of a sensual man.

Mrs Noronha, hunched up in her chair, head to one side, said in her way, 'A bad time. A bad decision. Much sorrow awaits you in Portugal. Your children will bring you much sorrow there.' But Carla, who two years before would have jumped with fright at such a message from the spirits, paid no attention; and she paid no attention when Mrs Noronha said it all a second time. The rest of us took our cue from Carla. We didn't interfere; we thought that what had happened or was happening between Carla and Mrs Noronha was a private matter. Mrs Noronha seemed to understand that she had overplayed her hand. She pressed her head into her neck, and in the beginning it looked as though anger and shame were going to send her away in a huff, as though at any moment she might make a gesture to her thin, sour-faced husband, the man of birth, and be wheeled out in disdainful

style from the company of the half-and-half people. It didn't
work out like that. Rather, over the hour and a half that
remained of the lunch, Mrs Noronha sought to play herself
back into the general conversation, making neutral or encour-
aging comments about many things, and in the end even
appearing to take an interest in Carla's arrangements in
Portugal. It was the beginning of the end for her as a sooth-
sayer – though she continued to appear among us for a few
more years. And it had been so easy to puncture her. It might
have been that, with the half-news and rumours that kept
on coming from the besieged frontiers, the racial and social
heights that the Noronhas represented no longer mattered as
much as they had.

It was only after we had left the lunch table that I came
face to face with Graça, the new manager's wife, Carla's
friend from the convent school. The first thing I noticed
about her was her light-coloured eyes: disturbed eyes; they
made me think again about her husband. And the second
thing I noticed was that, for a second or two, no more, those
eyes had looked at me in a way that no woman had looked
at me before. I had the absolute certainty, in that second, that
those eyes had taken me in not as Ana's husband or a man
of unusual origin, but as a man who had spent many hours
in the warm cubicles of the places of pleasure. Sex comes to
us in different ways; it alters us; and I suppose in the end we
carry the nature of our experience on our faces. The moment
lasted a second. It might have been fantasy, that reading of
the woman's eyes, but it was a discovery for me, something
about women, something to be added to my sensual education.

I met her again two weeks later, at a patriotic occasion in

the town, which began with a military parade in honour of a visiting general in the main square. It was a strange occasion, full of pomp and splendour, in which at the same time no one believed. It was an open secret that this conscript army, assembled here at such cost, no longer wanted to fight a war in Africa; it had become more concerned with conditions at home. And while at one time there was praise for the general who had devised the strategy of the wide sweep to the borders, now (when, from what we heard, it was already too late) it was said that the better strategy would have been to deploy the army on the border, in a chain of fortified areas, each fortified area with a strong mobile force that could combine with others at any given point. But on that Saturday morning all was still well with the army in the town. There were flags and speeches. The band played and the parade went on, and we all, young and old, Portuguese and Africans and people of the half-and-half world, merchants and loafers and beggar children, stood and watched and were carried away by the uniforms and the swords and the ceremonial, the music and the marching, the shouted orders and the complicated parade evolutions.

Afterwards there was the reception for the visiting general in the little governor's house in the town, opened up for the occasion. The governor's house was the oldest building in the town and one of the oldest in the colony. Some people said it was two hundred and fifty years old; but no one knew precisely. It was a stone-and-rubble building on two floors, square and plain, and from the outside it was perfectly ordinary. Perhaps in the old days governors had lived there or stayed there when they visited; but nobody lived in the governor's house now. It was a mixture of museum and historical monument, and the lower floor was open to the public one day a week. The two or three times I had been I hadn't seen anybody else, and there wasn't much to look at: a bleached but newish rowing boat that was said to be like the one Vasco da Gama had used when he came ashore here; and after that an assortment of old anchors, sometimes quite small, unexpectedly tall wooden rudders, put together from great planks and showing the skill of carpenters working with rough and heavy tools, winches, lengths of old rope: historical naval debris, like forgotten family junk, which no one wanted to throw away but which no one could identify and truly understand and honour.

It was different upstairs. I had never been there before. It was a grand dark room. The wide old floorboards, dark and rich with age, had a deep shine. The shutters, set far back in the thick walls, softened the light of sea and sky. On the faded, dark-painted ceiling there was some half-effaced decoration. All around the room were portraits of old governors, all the same size and all done in the same way – simple outlines, flat colours, with the name of each governor painted in mock old lettering at the top – suggesting a recent commission by some government cultural department; but somehow, perhaps because of the confidence and completeness of the arrangement, the idea worked; there was an effect of grandeur. The glory of the room, though, was the furniture. It was of ebony or some black wood and it was intricately carved, so intricately that each piece of wood seemed to have been hollowed out first and then carved on the front and the back. It was not furniture to sit on; it was furniture to look at, to see wood turned to lace, the furniture of the governor, a mark of his power. It was said to be as old as the house, and it all came, or so a Portuguese official standing beside me said, from Goa in Portuguese India. That was where all that pointless carving had been done.

So unexpectedly I found myself very close to home. I had been trying to take myself back two hundred and fifty years to the building of the governor's house, trying to find some footing in that unimaginable stretch of time, the sky always clear, the sea always blue and transparent except during the rains, the strange small ships appearing and then rocking at anchor some way out, the town hardly a settlement, the merest toehold on the coast, with no road inland to the rock cones, the local people there untouched – though it wouldn't have been like that: there would always have been some disturbance, something to send people to the fetish-man. I had been thinking like that, and then instead of Africa there had come India and Goa, and the cruel thought of those hands working for months or years on those extravagant chairs and settees for the governor here. It was like being given a new glimpse of our own history. Two hundred and fifty years: in certain parts of London that time would have been within reach, and romantic to re-create; in India, too, in the shadow of the great temple of our town; but here, in the governor's house, so far from everything, so far from history, it was terrible.

There would have been more than a hundred people in the room. Many of them were Portuguese, and I doubt whether any of them thought as I was thinking. The world was closing down for them in Africa; I don't think anyone there would have questioned that, in spite of all the speeches and the ceremonial; but they were all easy, enjoying the moment, filling the old room with talk and laughter, like people who didn't mind, like people who knew how to live with history. I never admired the Portuguese as much as I admired them then. I wished it was possible for me to live as easily with the past; but of course we were starting from opposite points.

And all this time I was thinking of Graça – Carla's convent-school friend, the wife of the new manager. I had been in the upstairs room for some time when I saw her. I hadn't seen her or her husband at the parade in the square, and wasn't looking for her here. It seemed to me a great piece of luck, a kind of gift, seeing her like this, when I wasn't looking for her. But I didn't want to force anything. I knew nothing about her apart from the little I had heard from Carla, and I might have misread her eyes. I thought it better, for greater security, to see whether accident wouldn't bring us together. And, slowly, accident did. We came together, she alone, I alone, in front of a Goan settee and an old Portuguese governor. I found again everything I had seen in her eyes. I was full of desire. Not the dumb, headlong, private desire of London, but a desire that came now from knowledge and experience and truly embraced the other person. At the same time I was quite shy. I could scarcely bear to look at her eyes. They promised such intimacies.

I said, 'I would like to see you.' She said, 'With my husband?' So he, poor man, was at once put out of the way. I said, 'You know that's a foolish question.' She said, 'When do you want to see me?' I said, 'Tomorrow, today. Any day.'

She pretended to take me literally. 'Today there's a big lunch here. Tomorrow there's going to be our Sunday lunch.' I said, 'I'll see you on Monday. Your husband will be going to the town to talk to government people about the price of cashew and cotton. Ask him to bring you to the house. It's on the way. We'll have a light lunch and then I'll drive you home. On the way we'll stop at the German Castle.' She said, 'When we were at the convent school we were sometimes taken there on an excursion. The Africans say it's haunted by the German who built it.'

After the Monday lunch I made no excuses to Ana. I had worked out none, and was ready for the worst if she objected. I simply said, 'I'll drive Graça home.' Ana said to Graça, 'I'm glad you're settling in.'

The German Castle was an abandoned estate house. I had gathered years before from various pieces of estate-house gossip that it was used for assignations. That was really all I was going by. It was an hour's fast drive, in a plain beyond the rock cones, which began at a certain stage to show in the distance as a joined-up range, low and blue. The plain was sandy and semi-fertile, and it looked empty, with villages hidden in the natural camouflage of sand and green. The Castle was on a slope in this apparent emptiness, and you could see it from far away. It was an enormous, extravagant estate house, wide and high, with a round concrete turret on either side of the front verandah. It was because of these turrets that the house was known as the Castle. The man who had built on such a scale in the wilderness must have thought he would never die, or he had misread history and thought he was leaving untold wealth to his descendants.

People didn't have dates for anything here; and no one knew for sure when the German Castle was built. Some people said it was built in the 1920s by a German settler from what had been German East Africa, coming after the 1914 war to friendlier Portuguese territory. Some people said it was built in the late 1930s by a German who wished to get away from Germany and the Depression and the coming war and hoped to create a self-sufficient estate here. But death had come; history had gone its own way; and long before my time – and again no one could tell me when – the Castle had been abandoned.

I drove the Land-Rover as far up the garden as it could go. What had been a big front garden with concrete-edged flowerbeds was bare and burnt away to sand, with scattered tufts of a hardy grass, a few long-stalked zinnias, and a purple bougainvillaea vine that had run wild. Wide and very smooth concrete steps, still unchipped, led to the verandah. The turret on either side had loopholes, as if for defence. Tall half-open doors showed the enormous dark drawing room. The floor was gritty. Some of that grit would have blown in with the wind; the bigger pieces might have been dropped by nest-building birds. There was a strange smell of fish; I took that to be the smell of a building in decay. I had brought an army rubber sheet with me. I spread it on the verandah, and without speaking we lay down on it.

The long drive had been a strain. Graça's need matched my own. That was new to me. Everything I had known before – the furtiveness of London, the awful provincial prostitute, the paid black girls of the places of pleasure here, who had yet satisfied me for so long, and for whom for almost a year I had felt such gratitude, and poor Ana, still in my mind the trusting girl who had sat on the settee in my college room in London and allowed herself to be kissed, Ana still so gentle and generous – over the next half-hour everything fell away, and I thought how terrible it would have been if, as could so easily have happened, I had died without knowing this depth of satisfaction, this other person that I had just discovered within myself. It was worth any price, any consequence.

I heard a voice calling. At first I couldn't be sure about it, but then I heard it as a man's voice calling from the garden. I put on my shirt and stood behind the verandah half-wall. It was an African, one of the eternal walkers on the ways, standing on the far edge of the garden, as though fearful of the house. When he saw me he made gestures and shouted, 'There are spitting cobras in the Castle.' That explained the smell of fish that had been with us: it was the smell of snakes.

We put on our clothes, wet as we were. We went down the wide, regal steps to the burnt-out sandy remains of the garden, very nervous there of the snakes that could blind from many feet. We finished dressing in the Land-Rover and drove away in silence. After a while I said to Graça, 'I am smelling you on my body as I drive.' I don't know how the courage came to me; but it seemed an easy and natural thing to say. She said, 'And I'm smelling you.' I loved her for that reply. I rested my right hand on her thigh for as long as I could, and I thought with sorrow – and now without personal shame – of my poor father and mother who had known nothing like this moment.

I began to arrange my life around my meetings with Graça, and I didn't care who noticed. With one part of my mind I was amazed at myself, amazed at the person I had become. A memory came to me of something that had happened at home, in the ashram, about twenty-five years before. I would have been about ten. A merchant of the town came to see my father. This merchant was rich and gave to religious charities, but people were nervous of him because he was said to be shameless in his private life. I didn't know what that meant but – together with the revolutionary teaching of my mother's uncle – it tainted the man and his riches for me. The merchant must have reached some crisis in his life; and, as a devout man, he had come to my father for advice and comfort. After the usual salutations and small talk, the merchant said, 'Master, I find myself in a difficult situation.' The merchant paused; my father waited. The merchant said, 'Master, I am like King Dasaratha.' Dasaratha was a sacred name; he was the ruler of the ancient kingdom of Kosala, and the father of the hero-divinity Rama. The merchant smiled, pleased at what he had said, pleased at easing himself with piety into his story; but my father was not pleased at all. He said in his severe way, 'How are you like King Dasaratha?' The merchant should have been warned by my father's tone, but he continued to smile, and said, 'Perhaps I am not quite like Dasaratha. He had three wives. I have two. And that, Master, is at the root of my troubles—' He was not allowed to say any more. My father said, 'How dare you compare yourself to gods? Dasaratha was a man of honour. His reign was of unparalleled righteousness. His later life was a life of sacrifice. How dare you compare yourself and your squalid bazaar lusts with such a man? If I were not a man of peace I would have you whipped out of my ashram.' The episode added to my father's reputation, and when, as now happened, we children found out about the shamelessness of the merchant's life, we were as appalled as my father. To have two wives and two families was to violate nature. To duplicate arrangements and affections was to be perpetually false. It was to dishonour everyone; it was to leave everyone standing in quicksand.

That was how it had looked to me when I was ten. Yet now every day I faced Ana without shame, and whenever I saw Luis, Graça's husband, I dealt with him with a friendship that was quite genuine, since it was offered out of gratitude for Graça's love.

I soon discovered that he was a drinking man, that the impression he had given at our first meeting of being a violent man who was holding himself in check had to do with his affliction. He drank right through the day, Graça told me, as though he had always to top up the energy that kept him going. He drank in small, undetectable quantities, a quick shot or two of rum or whisky, never more; and he never looked drunk or out of control. In fact, in company his drinking style made him seem almost abstemious. All Graça's married life had been dictated by this drinking of her husband's. They had moved from town to town, house to house, job to job.

She blamed the nuns for her marriage. At a certain stage in the convent school they had begun to talk to her about becoming a nun. They did that with girls who were poor; and Graça's family was poor. Her mother was a mixed-race person of no fortune; her father was second-rank Portuguese, born in the colony, who did a small job in the civil service. A religious charity had paid to send Graça to the convent, and it seemed to Graça that the nuns were now looking for some return. She was shy with them; she had always been an obedient child, at home and at school. She didn't say no; she didn't want to appear ungrateful. For months they tried to break her down. They praised her. They said, 'Graça, you are not a common person. You have special qualities. We need people like you to help lift the order up.' They frightened her, and when she went home for the holidays she was unhappier than she had ever been.

Her family had a small plot of land, perhaps two acres, with fruit trees and flowers and chickens and animals. Graça loved all of these things. They were things she had known since childhood. She loved seeing the hens sitting patiently on their eggs, seeing the fluffy little yellow chicks hatching out, cheeping, all of the brood being able to find shelter below the spread-out wings of the fierce, clucking mother hen, following the mother hen everywhere, and gradually, over a few weeks, growing up, each with its own colour and character. She loved having her cats follow her about in the field, and seeing them run very fast out of joy and not fear. The thought of cooping up these little creatures, cats or chickens, gave her great pain. The thought now of giving them all up for ever and being locked away herself was too much for her. She became frightened that the nuns would go behind her back to her mother, and her mother, religious and obedient, would give her away to them. That was when she decided to marry Luis, a neighbour's son. Her mother recognised her panic and agreed.

He had been after her for some time, and he was handsome. She was sixteen, he was twenty-one. Socially they were matched. She was more at ease with him than with the convent girls, most of whom were well-to-do. He worked as a mechanic for a local firm that dealt in cars and trucks and agricultural machinery, and he talked of setting up on his own. He was already a drinker; but at this stage it seemed only stylish, part of his go-ahead ways.

They moved after their marriage to the capital. He felt he was getting nowhere in the local town; he would never be able to start up on his own; the local rich people controlled everything and didn't allow the poor man to live. For a while in the capital they stayed with a relation of Luis's. Luis got a job as a mechanic in the railways, and then they were allocated a railway house that matched Luis's official grade. It was a small three-roomed house, one of a line, and built only to fit into that line. It was not built for the climate. It faced west; it baked every afternoon and cooled down only at about nine or ten in the evening. It was a wretched place to be in, day after day; it stretched everyone's nerves. Graça had her two children there. Just after the birth of her second child something happened in her head, and she found herself walking in a part of the capital she didn't know. At about the same time Luis was sacked for his drinking. That was when they started on their wandering life. Luis's skill as a mechanic kept them afloat, and there were times when they did very well. He still could charm people. He took up estate work and quickly became a manager. He was like that, always starting well and picking things up fast. But always, in every job, his resolve wore thin; some darkness covered his mind; there was a crisis, and a crash.

As much as by the life she had had with Luis, she was fatigued by the lies she had had to tell about him, almost from the beginning, to cover up his drinking. It had made her another kind of person. One afternoon she came back with the children from some excursion and they found him drinking home-made banana spirit with the African gardener, a terrible old drunk. The children were frightened; Graça had given them a horror of drinking. Now she had to think fast and say something different. She told them that what their father was doing was all right; times were changing, and it was socially just in Africa for an estate manager to drink with his African gardener. Then she found that the children were beginning to lie too. They had caught the habit from her. That was why, in spite of her own unhappiness at the convent, she had sent them to a boarding school.

For years she had dreamt of coming back to the country-side she knew as a child, where on her family's two-acre plot simple things, chickens and animals and flowers and fruit trees, had made her so happy in the school holidays. She had come back now; she was living as the manager's wife in an estate house with antique colonial furniture. It was a sham grandeur; things were as uncertain as they had ever been. It was as though the moods and stresses of the past would always be with her, as though her life had been decided long before.

This was what Graça told me about herself over many months. She had had a few lovers on the way. She didn't make them part of the main story. They occurred outside of that, so to speak, as though in her memory her sexual life was separate from her other life. And in this oblique way I learned that there had been people before me, usually friends of them both, and once even an employer of Luis's, who had read her eyes as I had read them, and spotted her need. I was jealous of all of these lovers. I had never known jealousy before. And thinking of all these people who had seen her weakness and pressed home their attack, I remembered some words of Percy Cato's in London, and for the first time had my own sense of the brutality of the sexual life.

I was deep in that brutality now with Graça. Sexual pictures of her played in my head when I was not with her. With her guidance, since she was the more experienced, our love-making had taken forms that had astonished, worried, and then delighted me. Graça would say, 'The nuns wouldn't approve of this.' Or she would say, 'I suppose if I went to confession tomorrow I would have to say, "Father, I've been immodest."' And it was hard to forget what she had taught, to unlearn the opening up of new senses; it was hard to go back to the sexual simplicities of earlier days. And I thought, as I often did on such occasions, of the puerility of my father's desires.

The months passed. Even after two years I felt myself helpless in this life of sensation. At the same time now some half-feeling of the inanity of my life grew within me, and with it there came the beginning of respect for the religious outlawing of sexual extremes.

Ana said to me one day, 'People are talking about you and Graça. You know that, don't you?'

I said, 'It's true.'

She said, 'You can't talk to me like this, Willie.'

I said, 'I wish you could be in the room when we make love. Then you would understand.'

'You shouldn't do this, Willie. I thought you at least had manners.'

I said, 'I'm talking to you like a friend, Ana. I have no one else to tell.'

She said, 'I think you've gone mad.'

And later I thought that perhaps she was right. I had talked out of a moment of sexual madness.

The next day she said, 'You know that Graça is a very simple person, don't you?'

I didn't know what she meant. Did she mean that Graça was poor, of no social standing, or did she mean that Graça was simple-minded?

She said, 'She's simple. You know what I mean.'

A little later she came back to me and said, 'I have a half-brother. Did you know that?'

'You never told me.'

'I would like to take you to see him. If you agree, I'll arrange it. I would like you to have some idea of what I've had to live with here, and why when I met you I thought I had met someone from another world.'

I felt a great pity for her, and also some worry about being punished for what I had done. I agreed to go and see her half-brother.

He lived in the African city on the edge of the town proper.

Ana said, 'You must remember he is a very angry man.

He wouldn't express this by shouting at you. He will show off. He will try to let you know that he doesn't care for you at all, that he's done well on his own.'

The African city had grown a lot with the coming of the army. It was now like a series of joined-up villages, with corrugated iron and concrete or concrete blocks taking the place of grass and cane. From a distance it looked wide and low and unnaturally level. Clumps of trees at the very edge marked the original shanty settlement, the city of cane, as people said. It was in that older African city that Ana's half-brother lived. Driving was not easy. The narrow lane we entered twisted all the time, and there was always a child carrying a tin of water on his head. In this dry season the dirt lane had been scuffed to red dust inches thick; and that dust billowed behind us and then around us like smoke. Runnels of dark waste from some yards were evaporating in the dust, and here and there were pools or dips of stagnant water. Some yards were fenced in with corrugated iron or cane. Everywhere there was green, shooting out of the dust, big, branching mango trees and slender paw-paw trees, with small plantings of maize and cassava and sugar-cane in many yards, almost as in a village. Some yards were workshops, making concrete blocks or furniture, patching up old tyres or repairing cars and trucks. Ana's half-brother was a mechanic, and he lived next to his big mechanic's yard. It looked busy, with many old cars and minibuses, and three or four men in very greasy shorts and singlets. The ground was black with old engine oil.

His house was better than most in the African city. It had no fence; it was built right up against the lane. It was low, of concrete, and it was carefully painted in yellow and green oil paint. The entrance was at the side. A very old black man, perhaps a servant, perhaps a distant relative, let us in. A wide verandah ran along the main rooms, which were on two sides of the yard. On the other two sides were separate buildings, servants' or visitors' quarters, perhaps, and the kitchen. All the buildings were linked by concrete walkways that were six inches or so above the thick dust (which would also turn into mud with rain). People were looking at us from the kitchen and the quarters, but the man himself came out to the verandah of the main house only when we were led there by the servant.

He was a dark man of medium height. He didn't look at Ana or at me. He was barefoot. He wore a singlet and very short and ragged shorts. Without looking at Ana he talked to her in a kind of mixed local language which was not easy for me to follow. She replied in the same language. Casually, dragging his soles on the concrete, he led us inside, into the formal room for visitors. A radio was going full blast; the radio was an important part of the furniture of this formal room. The windows were closed and the room was dark and very warm. I believe he offered to turn the air-conditioning on. Ana, as courteous as he was, told him he was not to bother. The room was stuffed with the formal furniture a room for visitors had to have: a set of upholstered chairs (these were covered in a shiny synthetic fabric), and a dining table with a full set of dining chairs (they were unpolished, raw-looking, and might have been made in one of the furniture workshops in the lane). There wasn't really room for everything; everything was jammed together. All the time he talked, showing Ana what he had, without looking at her, and all the time Ana was complimenting him. He invited us to sit on the upholstered chairs. Ana, matching his courtesy, said we would prefer to sit outside; and so, turning off the radio, he went back with us to the wide verandah, where there were everyday chairs and tables.

He shouted, and a very small white woman came from one of the rooms. She had a blank, full face; she was not young. He introduced this woman, his wife, as I now understood, to Ana; and Ana was gracious. The small white woman – and she was very small indeed, not much taller than the glass-walled cabinet (with ornaments) against which she leaned – asked us to drink something. Immediately there was shouting in the kitchen. The man sat down in a low armchair. He used his feet to pull a stool towards him and he rested his feet on the stool, with his knees wide apart; his ragged shorts fell back almost to his crotch. All the time people in the yard, in the kitchen and the quarters, were looking at us; but he still didn't look at Ana or me. I saw now that, dark though he was, his eyes were light. He stroked the inside of his thighs slowly, as though he was caressing himself. Ana had prepared me for this kind of aggression; it would have been hard for me otherwise. And quite late I saw that, apart from his wife and the cabinet of ornaments, he had another treasure on the verandah: a big green-tinted bottle with a living snake, on an oilcloth-covered table just beside his chair.

The snake was greenish. When the man tormented it or teased it the snake, tightly imprisoned though it was, lashed out with frightening abrupt wide-mouthed rage against the side of the bottle, which was already discoloured with some kind of mucus from the snake's mouth. The man was pleased with the effect the snake had on me. He began to talk to me in Portuguese. For the first time he looked at me. He said, 'It's a spitting cobra. They can blind you from fifteen feet. They aim for shiny things. They will aim for your watch or your glasses or your eyes. If you don't wash it off fast with sugar and water you are in trouble.'

On the way back I said to Ana, 'It was terrible. I was glad you told me about the showing off. I didn't mind that. But the snake – I wanted to break that bottle.'

She said, 'My own flesh and blood. To think of him there all the time. That's what I've had to live with. I wanted you to see him. It is what you might leave behind.'

* * *

I LET IT PASS. I had no wish to quarrel with her. She had been very good and delicate with her half-brother, very good in a bad situation; and old love and regard for her had welled up in me. Old love: it was still there, it could even be added to at moments like this, but it belonged now to another life, or a part of my life that had run its course. I no longer slept in her grandfather's big carved bed; but we lived easily in the same house, often ate together, and had many things to talk about. She no longer sought to rebuke me. Sometimes when we were talking she would pull herself up and say, 'But I shouldn't be talking to you like this.' And a little while later she would start again. On estate matters and the doings of estate people I continued to trust her.

And I wasn't surprised when news came that Carla Correia was selling her estate. Ana had always said that this was what

Carla was going to do; that in spite of the talk of charity to a school friend, Luis and Graça had been put in the estate house only to keep it in good order until it could be sold. Carla had sold to a big property company in Portugal, and she had sold at the top. Estate prices, which had been falling because of the guerrilla war in the north and west, had risen again, in an irrational way, because certain influential people in Lisbon had begun to say that the government and the guerrillas were about to come to an agreement.

So Luis and Graça were going to be on the move again. The property company wanted the estate house for their own directors when they came out 'on tour' (the company apparently believed that the colonial order, and colonial style, were going to continue after the war). But things were not all bad for Luis and Graça. The company wanted Luis to stay on as estate manager. They were going to build a new house for him on a two-acre plot; and after a few years Luis would be able to buy the house on easy terms. Until the house was built Luis and Graça would continue to live in the estate house. It was part of the deal Carla had made with the company. So Ana was both right and wrong. Carla had (in a small way) used Luis and Graça to add to her fortune, but she had not forgotten her school friend. Graça was very happy. Since she had left home she had never had a house of her own. It was what she had dreamt about for years, the house and the garden and the fruit trees and the animals. She had begun to think it would never come, but now in a roundabout way it had.

Very soon after the sale the property company, doing things in its grand way, sent out an architect from the capital to build Graça's house. She could scarcely believe her luck.

An architect, and from Portugal! He stayed in one of the guest rooms in the estate house. His name was Gouveia. He was informal and metropolitan and stylish, and he made everyone in our area seem old-fashioned. He wore very tight jeans that made him look a little heavy and soft; but we didn't think of criticising. He was in his thirties, and everybody in the estate-house circle fawned on him. He began to come to our Sunday lunches. We assumed that because he came from Portugal and was working for the property company, which was buying up old estates, gambling on the past continuing, we assumed that he would speak against the guerrillas. But he did the other thing. He spoke with relish of the blood to come, almost in the way Jacinto Correia used to talk in the old days. We decided he was a white man pretending to be a black man. It was a type we were just beginning to get in the colony, playboy figures, well-to-do, full Portuguese, people like Gouveia, in fact, who could cut and run or look after themselves if there was any real trouble.

After a week or so word got around that Gouveia had a liaison with an African woman in the capital. As always when new people came it was as though somebody was doing research, and in the next few days we began to hear stories about this woman. One story was that she had gone with Gouveia to Portugal, but had refused to do any housework because she didn't want people in Portugal to think she was a servant. Other stories were about her servants in the capital. In one story the servants were always quarrelling with her because she was an African and they had no regard for her. In another story somebody asked her why she was so hard on her servants, and she said she was an African and knew how to deal with Africans. The stories sounded made-up; they looked back to the past, and no one really believed them or found comfort in them; but they did the rounds. And then the woman came from the capital to be with Gouveia for a few days, and he brought her to the Sunday lunch. She was perfectly ordinary, blank-faced, assessing, self-contained and silent, a village woman transported to the town. After a while we saw that she was pregnant, and then we were all ourselves like mice. Afterwards somebody said, 'You know why he is doing that, don't you? He wants to curry favour with the guerrillas. He feels that if he has an African woman with him when they come they won't kill him.'

We made love in the house, Graça and I, as it was being built. She said, 'We must christen all the rooms.' And we did. We carried away the smell of planed wood and sawdust and new concrete. But other people were also attracted to the new house. One day, hearing talk, we looked out of a half-made wall and saw some children, innocent, experienced, frightened to see us. Graça said, 'Now we have no secrets.'

One day we found Gouveia. I could see in his dark shining eyes that he had read our purpose. He explained in a showing-off way what he was aiming to do with Graça's house. Then he said, 'But I want to live in the German Castle. Houses have their destiny, and the destiny of the Castle is that it shall belong to me. I'll do it up in the most fabulous way, and when the revolution comes I'll move there.' I thought of the house and the view and the German and the snakes and he said, 'Don't look so frightened, Willie. I'm only quoting *Zhivago*.'

Early one night, when the lights were still jumping, Ana came to my room. She was distressed. She was in her short nightdress that emphasised her smallness and the fineness of her bones.

She said, 'Willie, this is so terrible I don't know how I can talk about it. There's excrement on my bed. I discovered it just now. It's Júlio's daughter. Come and help with the sheets. Come and let's burn everything.'

We went to the big carved bed and stripped it fast. The lights blinked; and Ana became more and more distressed. She said, 'I feel so dirty. I feel I have to bathe and bathe.'

I said, 'Go and have a shower. I'll burn the sheets.'

I took the great bundle down to the dead part of the garden. I poured gasoline on it and threw a match at it from a distance. The flame roared up, and I watched it burn it down, while the generator hummed and the lights in the house dipped and rose.

It was a bad night. She came to my room, wet and shivering from the shower, and I held her. She allowed herself to be held, and I thought again of the way she had allowed herself to be kissed in my college room in London. I also thought of Júlio's daughter, who as a young girl had tried to make polite conversation with me; who had stolen my passport and papers; and whom I had seen but not acknowledged in one of the places of pleasure.

Ana said, 'I don't know whether she put it there. Or whether she squatted on the bed.'

I said, 'Don't think like that. Just think that you're getting rid of her in the morning.'

She said, 'I want you to stand by in the morning. Don't show yourself, but stand by, in case she turns violent.'

In the morning Ana was composed again. When Júlio's

daughter came, Ana said, 'That was a vile thing to do. You've been in this house since you were born. You are a vile person. I should have you whipped by your father. But all I want is that you should leave now. You have half an hour.'

Júlio's daughter said, with the pertness she had picked up in the places of pleasure, 'I am not vile. You know who's vile.'

Ana said, 'Get out and don't come back. You have half an hour.'

Júlio's daughter said, 'It's not for you to tell me not to come back. I may come back one day, and sooner than you think. And I'll not be staying in the quarters then.'

I had been standing in the bathroom behind the half-opened door. I felt that Júlio's daughter knew I was there, and I thought, as I had been thinking all night, 'Ana, what have I done to you?'

At our Sunday lunch that week there was a man from the local mission who had come back from the mission's outposts in the north. He said, 'People here and in the capital know nothing of the war in the bush. Life here has gone on just as it has always done. But there are whole areas in the north now where the guerrillas rule. They have schools and hospitals, and they are arming and training the village people.' Gouveia said, in his joking way, 'And when do you think we'll be hearing the crump of artillery in the hot tropical night?' The missionary said, 'The guerrillas are probably all around you. They never attack settled areas in the way you say. They send unarmed people. They look like ordinary Africans. They spread the word of revolution. They prepare the people.' And I thought of my impressions of the very first day, of Africans walking, and the later impression of the estates and the settlements of concrete being in an African sea. Gouveia said, 'You mean I can be held up on the road now?' The missionary said, 'It's possible. They're all around us.' Gouveia said, only half joking now, 'I think I shall try to leave before the airport closes down.'

Mrs Noronha said in her prophesying voice, 'Hoard cloth. We must hoard cloth.' Somebody said, 'Why should we do that?' No one since Carla Correia had spoken like that to Mrs Noronha. Mrs Noronha said, 'We are now like the Israelites in the desert.' Somebody said, 'I've never heard of the Israelites hoarding cloth.' And poor Mrs Noronha, all her mystical credit gone, recognising that she had confused her prophecies, pressed her head against her shoulder and closed her eyes and was wheeled out of our lives. We heard later, after the handover to the guerrillas, that she was one of the first to be repatriated to Portugal.

Well before that handover Graça's house was finished. She and Luis gave a housewarming. They had very little furniture. But Luis carried off the occasion with his style as a host, bending forward almost in a confiding way to offer a drink. Two weeks later he and his Land-Rover disappeared. The colonial police, at that time still in control, said he had probably been kidnapped by the guerrillas. No official in our town had any contact with the guerrillas, so there was no means of finding out more. Graça was wild with grief. She said, 'He was full of despair. I can't tell you how full of despair he was ever since we moved into the house. He should have been happy, but it worked the other way.' And then some days later some herdsmen found him and the Land-Rover well off the dirt road, near a cattle pond. The door of the Land-Rover was open, and there were bottles of drink.

He was almost naked, but still alive. His mind had gone, or so the report suggested. All he could do was to repeat words spoken to him. 'You went out on a spree?' And he said, 'Spree.' 'Did the guerrillas pick you up?' And he said, 'Guerrillas.' They brought him back to the new, empty house. Graça was waiting for him. My mind went back years to the mission school and a poem in the third-standard reader:

> *Home they brought her warrior dead.*
> *She nor swooned nor uttered cry.*
> *All her maidens watching said,*
> *'She must weep or she will die.'*

We never made love again.

She looked after him in the new house. It was her new role, being his nurse, tending him like a nun of a service order. If there wasn't a war there might have been a doctor who would have known what to do. But people like doctors were leaving the colony or country every day; the estate was far out; the road was dangerous; and Luis with his ruined brain and liver just faded away in the empty house.

Great events in the life of the colony, the final rites, happened at a distance from her. The colonial government in the capital closed down, just like that; the guerrillas took over. The Portuguese population began to leave. The army withdrew from our town. The barracks were empty; it seemed unnatural, after the activity and the daily military rituals, like church rituals, of the past twelve years. And then after some weeks of this blankness a much smaller force of guerrillas moved in, occupying just a part of the barracks that had been extended many times during the war. People had died, but the army hadn't really wished to fight this African war, and life in the towns remained normal right up to the end. The war was like a distant game; even at the end it was hard to believe that the game was going to have great consequences. It was as though the army, with some political purpose, had colluded with the guerrillas (with their tactic of unarmed infiltration) to preserve the peace of towns; so that when the time came the guerrillas would be able to take over towns in working order.

For a while, as after the application of herbicide, nothing showed, and it was possible to think that nothing had changed, that goods would continue to come to the shops, and gasoline to the pumps. But then, all at once, as with herbicide, the change showed. Certain shops became empty and then didn't reopen; their owners had gone away, to South Africa or Portugal. Some houses in the central square were abandoned. Very quickly light globes on gate posts or in verandahs were broken; a short while later glass panes, which had remained intact for years, mysteriously dropped away; then windows were taken off their hinges; and here and there rafters began to rot and tile roofs sagged. We had thought that the municipal services of our little town were rudimentary. Now we felt their absence. Street drains became blocked, and glaciers of sand (with patches of wild grass on the high parts, and rippled or plaited patterns of fine sand in the miniature watercourses that ran after rain) inched their way out of drives into choked gutters. Gardens became overgrown and then as burnt-out as the formal gardens of the German Castle, which had been abandoned for three decades; in the climate everything speeded up and became what it had to be. In the countryside the main asphalt road was dreadfully potholed. Some estate houses lost their owners, and African families, shy at first of people like Ana, began to move into the wide verandahs behind the bougainvillaea vines.

There were hard months. Mrs Noronha, in the last days of order, had asked us to hoard cloth for the bad times to come. We hoarded gasoline. The estate had its own pump; we filled jerricans and hid them; without our Land-Rovers we would have been lost. We stopped running our generators. So our nights became silent; and we discovered the charm of the big shadows cast by an oil lamp. It didn't take long for things to break down, to become again as they had been in the days of Ana's grandfather, who had had to live close to the ground, close to the climate and insects and illnesses, and close to his African neighbours and workers, before comfort had been squeezed out of the hard land, like blood out of stone.

In her house Graça managed quite well. In a way it was what she had always wanted: a house and two acres, and hens and fruit trees. She was readier than Ana was to welcome the new régime.

She said, 'They want us to live in a sharing way. It is the better life. You see, the nuns were right after all. The time has come for us all to be poor. We have to share everything we have. They are right. We have to be as everybody else. We have to serve and be useful. I will give them all that I have. I will not let them ask. I will give them this house.' Her two children had gone with many of her relatives to Portugal. 'I was angry with them. In Portugal they will have to prepare papers to say who they are. How can anyone do that? How can anyone say who he is? They will prepare papers to say they are Portuguese. I don't have to do that here. My grandfather is buried here. He died young. He is among the ancestors. I go to his grave every year to talk to him. I talk about the family. I tell him everything. I feel good when I do that. Of course, I don't tell people. They think I'm going to the market.'

I looked at her suffering eyes and thought, 'I was making love to a deranged woman. Can it be true, what I felt I had with her?'

Ana said, when I told her, 'She is not giving them anything. Even in her grief she is fooling herself. They are taking it from her. They say they are going to take it all away from me, too. But I'm not running away. Half of what my grandfather gave me was stolen by my father. I will stay here and protect the other half. I do not want people squatting in my house or sleeping in my bed.'

In time the new government put together a kind of administration. Everything took three or four times as long as it did before, but we learned how to get things done. There were services of a sort again. The great hardship was over. But just at this time there were rumours of a new, tribal war. Just as the anti-Portuguese guerrillas had begun in the bush, so now the people hostile to the victors were beginning in the bush. The guerrillas had had the support of the black governments over the border. The new insurgents had the support of the white government to the west, and they were far more deadly. It was their policy to 'blood' new recruits, to get a recruit to kill someone. They raided the outskirts of towns and killed people and burnt houses and spread terror.

I didn't think I could live through another war. I could see that it would have a point for Ana. I didn't see that it had a point for me. For some weeks I was perplexed. I didn't know what to do. I suppose I didn't have the courage to tell Ana. It was the rainy season. I had cause to remember it. The heavy pollen from the shade tree in front of the estate house made the semi-circular marble steps slippery. I slipped and fell heavily. When I awoke, in the run-down military hospital in the barracks in the town, the physical pain of my damaged body was like the other pain that had been with me for months, and perhaps for years.

When Ana came to the hospital courage came to me, and I told her I wanted to divorce her.

When she came back later I said to her, 'I am forty-one. I am tired of living your life.'

'You wanted it, Willie. You asked. I had to think about it.'

'I know. You did everything for me. You made it easy for me here. I couldn't have lived here without you. When I asked you in London I was frightened. I had nowhere to go. They were going to throw me out of the college at the end of the term and I didn't know what I could do to keep afloat. But now the best part of my life has gone, and I've done nothing.'

'You are frightened of the new war.'

'And even if we go to Portugal, even if they let me in there, it would still be your life. I have been hiding for too long.'

Ana said, 'Perhaps it wasn't really my life either.'

March 1999–August 2000

picador.com

blog
videos
interviews
extracts